The Facts Speak for Themselves

Also by Brock Cole

THE GOATS

CELINE

BROCK COLE

The Facts Speak for Themselves

YOUNG PICADOR

First published 1997 by Front Street Books

This edition published 2002 by Young Picador
An imprint of Pan Macmillan Ltd
Pan Macmillan, 20 New Wharf Road, London, N1 9RR
Basingstoke and Oxford
Associated companies throughout the world
www.panmacmillan.com

ISBN 0330 400975

1 3 5 7 9 8 6 4 2

A CIP catalogue record for this book is available from
the British Library.

Phototypeset by Intype London Ltd
Printed and bound in Great Britain by Mackays of Chatham plc, Kent

For Marion

If you need to talk to someone about any of the issues raised in this book, ChildLine is the free, national helpline for children and young people. It provides a confidential phone counselling service for any child with any problem twenty-four hours a day, every day.

You can contact ChildLine on 0800 1111, or write to ChildLine, Freepost 1111, London N1 0BR.

Website: http://www.childline.org.uk
e-mail: info@childline.org.uk

1

The woman policeman says why don't you come in here, and so I went. It was a little room with a table and some chairs. That was all. Instead of a window, there was a big mirror. I wouldn't look at that. I didn't want to see myself. I sat down and folded my hands. There was still blood under my nails, so after a minute I put them under the table.

The woman says would you like something to drink? A Coke or something?

No, I don't want anything.

We're trying to locate your mother right now. We'll just wait here until she comes.

Oh, I said.

Is that all right?

Yes. That's all right.

The other policeman came in. The one with the white hair and the stomach.

He says well how are you, Linda.

I'm OK.

He spreads some papers out in front of him but can't find what he's looking for.

He says how old are you?

Thirteen.

Thirteen?

Yes, I said.

We haven't been able to locate your mother, Linda. She works for Persic Realty. Is that right?

Yes.

We called there, and the woman who answered the phone said she didn't come in today and she doesn't respond to her pager. We sent a car over to your apartment and she's not there either. Did she tell you where she might be going today? Did you forget? Do you know where she is now?

No, I don't know. I thought she'd be at Persic's.

When did you see your mother last, Linda?

This morning.

Well, did she say where she was going?

No. She was asleep when I left.

I changed Tyler's diaper and took him in and put him in her bed. I'm going now, I said. You're going to have to take Tyler to day care yourself today. I'll put Stoppard on his school bus. Do you understand what I'm telling you?

The policeman told the woman to get out her notebook.

Would you mind going over what happened on the parking ramp once more for me, Linda? he said.

I already told the other policeman.

I understand that, but I'd like you to explain it to me yourself.

I knew he would say that. I already knew I was going to have to tell what happened over and over.

I started. We were standing on the ramp talking, I say.

2

Already he has to interrupt. That was you and Mr Green?

Yes.

What were you and Mr Green talking about?

I don't remember. It was about what we could see from the parking ramp. That was all. He said he couldn't decide if the world would look any different if it was flat instead of round. He said a person walking away from us would disappear. Because of the curve. First his feet and finally his head. If the earth was flat and there was nothing in the way, he would just get smaller and smaller.

What happened then?

Frank came up and shot him.

Frank is Mr Perry?

Yes. Frank Perry.

You knew Mr Perry?

Yes. We lived with him for a while.

We? You mean your mother and you?

Yes. And the boys.

He was your mother's friend?

Yes.

I see.

The policeman stopped and wrote that down himself on a paper.

Was he on foot or in a car?

On foot. If he had his car I didn't see it.

I see. Did you know he was going to be there? At the parking ramp?

No, I didn't know. I didn't even see him until he came up and stuck the gun in Jack and shot him.

Jack is Mr Green? You call him Jack?

Yes.

Before he shot Mr Green . . . did Mr Perry say anything?

Yes. He said you son of a bitch and then he shot him. It was all at the same time.

What happened then?

Nothing. Jack held on to me. He was afraid of falling down, I think. I tried to hold him up, but he was too heavy. He sat down finally on the cement and held his stomach.

What did Mr Perry do after he shot Mr Green?

He didn't do anything. He just stood there.

Did he say anything?

He might have said he was sorry. I'm not sure. Then he walked away.

Do you know where he went?

No, I don't know.

What did you do then?

I told Jack I was going to call 911, but he said no, don't go.

Did you stay with him?

Yes. That woman with the little boy came right after, and she went to call the ambulance.

Did Mr Green say anything else?

Like what?

Like anything. Any words.

No.

I see, the policeman says. The woman policeman closes up her notebook, and they look at each other as if they are thinking the same thing. After a minute they both go away. I learned later a person can see through that mirror from the other side, so one of the other officers kept an eye on me until Miss Jessop from Children's Protective Services came.

4

It was Miss Jessop who told me that I wasn't going home after all. They were going to send me to the Centre pending further investigation into my family circumstances.

I gave her an argument. Oh, that's great. What about Stoppard and Tyler? Who's going to take care of them?

Those are your brothers?

Yes. Those are my brothers. Tyler's at day care.

I lean over and look at her watch.

Stoppard's probably already at Tiny Tots wondering where I am.

She writes down the name of the lady who takes care of Tyler during the day and Stoppard's school.

What are you going to do? Are they going to come to the Centre, too?

That's a possibility. We have to see if your mother is in a position to take care of them.

Oh, that's a great idea. Why don't you just put Mom in the Centre and let me go home? That would be a lot simpler.

Now that's enough, Miss Jessop tells me.

She drove me over to the Centre in her car. I took one look. There was a big cross in front with Jesus hanging on it.

I said this is for Catholics.

No, not just for Catholics. It's run by Catholic charities, but you're welcome here even if you're not a Catholic.

She handed me over to a Sister in the office. Her name is Sister Mary Joseph. She came out from behind a wood counter and shook hands.

Hello, Linda, she says. I've been waiting for you. I

thought maybe you and I could have some lunch, but maybe you want to get cleaned up first.

Yes, I say. Yes.

In the halls there wasn't anybody else.

Where are the other kids? I said.

They're in school. You want to take a shower? I have some clean clothes for you. They're too big, but nobody said how little you are. They'll do for right now.

She didn't ask any personal questions. I suppose the police had called and told her all there was to know, but still I was relieved not to have to make any explanation.

She helped me get my clothes off. My shirt was stuck to my chest with blood, and when I pushed my jeans down, I saw it had soaked right through to my underwear.

It was when I was naked that I let loose and start to cry.

Sister Mary Joseph says I know, Linda. I know. She gives me a brush for my nails and a bar of soap and turns on the water. It comes out steaming hot. It's what I want.

Take your time, she says. I'll be right outside in case you need anything.

After my shower I didn't want lunch. I was tired and I wanted to lie down somewhere.

Sister Mary Joseph showed me my room. This is where you'll sleep, she says.

There were four beds, but only three made up. The one for me had an army blanket and was far from the window. I stripped down to my underwear again and got between the sheets.

Sister Mary Joseph says you call if you want anything.

All right, I said.

6

It was still light out. I couldn't close my eyes. I lay in the bed and felt the sheets. They were rough and stiff but clean. I could see the sky through the window. After a while a girl comes into the room and looks at me. She's got on a plaid skirt, and one of her ears is torn.

I have to get something out of my locker, she says. Is that OK?

I open my mouth to say OK, but nothing comes out, so I just nod.

She gets a book out of a grey locker and goes away. After she's gone I can smell her in the air for a second. She has a clean smell, like the sheets.

The next thing it was dark and the lights were on and there were two girls in the room getting ready for bed. One was the girl with the torn ear. The other was pink and blonde. I lie still and look at the girl with the ear. She takes off her top. She's the same greeny yellow colour all over. On her the colour looks good.

She's awake, says the other one.

The girl with the ear looks at me. Are you OK?

Yes. Yes, I'm OK.

She goes and gets something wrapped up in a paper napkin out of her locker. She sits down on my bed and opens it up. Inside is a cloverleaf roll with a polished brown top like the toe of a shoe.

I thought you might want something to eat.

Thanks, I say, and eat.

I can go down to the kitchen and get you some other stuff if you're hungry. Sister Mary Joseph said I could get you anything you want.

No, I say. This is all I want.

I couldn't eat any more, so I lay still and watched them

7

get into bed. They talked about a concert the school was putting on for the elderly. What kind of concert, I wondered, but I was too tired to ask.

The girl with the ear says tomorrow I'm going to ask Miss Thompson if I can sing in the jazz choir. It's more interesting. She looks at me while she talks. She looks at my hair and my eyes. My mouth. It made me feel I was nice to look at. I closed my eyes then and went back to sleep.

The next morning I had breakfast in the cafeteria with the other girls. When I went through the line I waited to see what they got, and then I got the same thing. Scrambled eggs and fruit cup.

Sister Mary Joseph comes up to our table and says Linda you slept for nearly sixteen hours. She says do you want to go to school with the other girls?

No. I got my own school, I told her. Arthur Murray Middle School.

The question made me wonder who was taking care of Tyler and Stoppard. That woman from Protective Services, Miss Jessop, said she'd look after things, but what if she forgot? She just wrote something on a piece of paper and stuck it in her briefcase. I wouldn't like my life to depend on that.

I said I wonder if I can make a phone call.

Who to?

I want to call Mom and see if everything's OK.

Sister Mary Joseph said that's not possible at the moment. Why don't you go with Crystal and Beverly to school for the day? she says. You might like it.

I got argumentative then, but it was because I was thinking about Tyler and Stoppard.

No, I say. I told you I've got my own school. I want to know if things are OK at home. Would you please explain to me why I can't use the fucking phone for two minutes?

I said you can't stop me.

That was out of line. Way out. Sister Mary Joseph caught me round the waist and carried me over to the side of the room. She sat down on a chair there with me on her lap and wrapped her arms and legs around me so I couldn't move.

I fought her for a minute, but she was too strong.

What's the problem? said another woman. She was a Sister, too. You could tell because she wore the outfit. Sister Mary Joseph just wore regular clothes.

Linda blew her top, Sister Mary Joseph said. She made it sound like a joke. I tried to break out again, but somehow all the strength went out of me.

When I got calmed down I explained my worries about Tyler and Stoppard, and Sister Mary Joseph said she'd make inquiries.

I don't see why I can't just call, I said.

Don't start again, Linda. I said I'd find out how they are, and you'll just have to be satisfied with that.

The other girls went to their school, but I went up to the office with Sister Mary Joseph and sat there most of the day. We had lunch on a tray together in her own room. It was macaroni and cheese with two cookies in a plastic wrap. Later I was sitting on a bench in the hall when the Sister in the outfit came up and told me that Tyler and Stoppard were fine. Her name is Sister Angelica. She said the boys were staying with Mom for the moment,

9

but she was getting some help in dealing with the situation.

What kind of help, I start. I don't think she can take care of anything without me.

Listen, young lady, Sister says. You're not in charge any more. This is a difficult situation, and it's going to take a little time to straighten out. Two men are dead, she says and bites her lip.

What two men?

Mr Green and Mr Perry.

That was how I found out. Jack had died in the ambulance and Frank had walked down into the basement of the parking ramp and shot himself.

She had to explain herself to Sister Mary Joseph for spilling the beans like that.

I thought she knew, she says.

She starts to cry. She says Linda never asked about either one and so I just assumed she knew.

That was her excuse for telling me the news cold like that in the hall.

I didn't feel anything. What she said was true. I'd never asked anybody if Jack was all right or what happened to Frank Perry. Maybe I already did know. I think I knew Jack was dead as soon as the ambulance came.

When Sister Mary Joseph sent the other Sister out of the room, she didn't make a big deal of the situation.

It would have been better if you'd found out some other way, but on the scale of big mistakes this doesn't register very high. You understand, Linda?

She gave me the details later about what happened to Frank. He walked down the parking ramp, right past his truck, to the very bottom. When he couldn't go down any more, he stood against the wall that was stopping him and shot himself in the head.

Two women in suits showed up and said they had to talk to me. I didn't like those. One wore her suit right over her underwear without any blouse. I gave them the statement about what happened. It was pretty much what I'd told the policeman, but they wanted all the details. All sorts of things that didn't have much to do with whose fault it was. Every time I answered a question they would look at each other.

Mr Green was a family friend?

What do you mean?

Was your family friends with his?

He and Mom worked at the same place.

So you saw him pretty often, I suppose.

Yes. Pretty often.

Did you ever see him alone?

Sometimes.

Were you intimate with Mr Green?

I pretend I don't even hear questions like that.

Linda? Did you hear what I asked you?

Yes. Yes, I heard.

Were you having sexual relations with Mr Green?

I look out the window at the birds in the trees.

Would you answer the question please?

After a while Sister Mary Joseph tells them to go away. I watch them from the window, swishing their butts. They get into a big car and one dials up a carphone while the other one drives. I look at Sister Mary Joseph over my shoulder. She's watching me and tapping her teeth with a pencil.

Those are hookers, I say. You shouldn't let hookers in the Centre.

She puts down her pencil and spreads out her fingers on the blotter.

Linda, she says. You're going to have to tell somebody. You understand that, don't you? You're never going to get out of here until they find out all they want to know.

I don't talk to any hookers.

I tell her that.

I don't talk to fucking hookers.

That afternoon Franny Paschonelle showed up. She's my social worker.

She says I meant to get here two days ago, but my car broke down.

Sister Mary Joseph's eyebrows go up.

Miss Paschonelle arranged for me to get some tests to find out about my personality, and I saw a doctor.

Then Miss Paschonelle and me took a walk.

She says I want to be straight with you, Linda. We have to decide whether to put you in foster care or not. You and your brothers. So you're going to have to tell me what's been going on in your life. I mean about your mom. I mean about Mr Green and Mr Perry. Everything. Are you ready to do that?

She had a big bag slung on her shoulder bursting with papers, and her clothes kept slipping down. It was as if she had on her big sister's stuff. She smelled like sweat and cigarettes, but she was OK.

I asked her if she had a boyfriend.

No!

She barks like a happy dog.

I was married once. For two months. Wasn't that a joke! But we're not here to talk about me. Are you going to tell me everything or not? If not, I got a million other things to do.

All right, I say. I'll talk to you.

I gave her the facts, and she wrote them up in a preliminary report. I know, because I got it out of her bag when she came back one afternoon to warn me about what was going to happen.

There's going to be a hearing, she says, and I want you to be as straight with the judge as you are with me.

I fished the report out when she went to use the toilet.

I could hear her talking to Sister Angelica in the hall, so I knew I had plenty of time to look things over.

The subject is female, age thirteen. Her mother is Caucasian and her father, now deceased, was Native American. Her score on the standard Stanford-Binet puts her in the low-average range of her age group. She appears to be in good physical health (see attached physician's report). She is small for her age, but sturdily built. She reports that her onset of menses occurred seven months ago. Her periods are scanty and irregular. Sexually active . . . repeatedly molested by her mother's employer . . . no evidence of collusion on the mother's part . . . evidently very distraught . . .

When she came back in the room I didn't try to hide what I was doing. She takes the paper out of my hand and sits down across the table.

She says I thought I could trust you, Linda.

I knew that was talk. She was afraid because she'd been careless and let me get hold of the report.

I said if you trusted me, you'd let me read the paper.

I can't do that. I can't make an objective report if I know you're going to see it.

You want me to trust you, but you can say what you want behind my back.

That isn't the way it is, Linda.

You make me look like a fool.

I did? She leafs through the pages. It's all true, isn't it? Isn't this what you told me?

You make me look like a stupid fool.

She closes up the folder and puts her hands on it.

It was a touchy situation, and we stared grimly at each other.

I want to write my own preliminary report, I said.

She looked at me a long time.

I think that's a very good idea, she says finally.

Will they read it?

Yes, she says. I'll make sure they do.

2

Miss Paschonelle asked me if I have my own room, so I will begin there.

I do have my own room. I keep Tyler in there with me most nights, but still it's my room. I have a bed and a table for homework. It's got a drawer for supplies, and there is a bookcase on one side where I can set stuff that won't go in the drawer. I keep my clothes in a cardboard box in the closet. I've got two cardboard boxes. One for clean clothes and the other for dirty. I can tell at a glance when it's time to do the laundry. We do our laundry at Wash 'n Dry. It costs a dollar a load to wash. The dryer takes quarters. I put in seventy-five cents to start and then add another if the clothes aren't dry enough. They also have a wash-and-fold service for eighty-nine cents a pound. If you choose that option, Mrs Hubble will go through all the motions with the machine and dryer and then fold the clothes up on a white table and slip them in a plastic bag.

When Mrs Hubble washes other people's clothes, she has to put quarters in the machine like anyone else. She keeps them in a Folger's coffee can on a shelf in the store-room. That's where I got the idea for having a can at home. My can is blue. It is a Maxwell House can. I put it on the back of the sink first, but it made a round rust spot there, so I moved it to the cup cupboard. I told Mom to put any quarters she has in her purse into the can when she comes home, and that way we'll always have enough to do the laundry. She doesn't do it unless I remind her, and sometimes she takes them out again when I'm not looking. Still, I think it's a good idea.

Tyler doesn't have a baby bed. He sleeps in his playpen, which is made out of net stretched over some chrome pipes. This is a perfectly satisfactory arrangement. He has a walking blanket, and I put him in that, and then he can crawl all over the bottom of the pen in his sleep and still be warm. There is a place between the foot of my bed and the window where the playpen just fits, so that's where I put it. If he wakes up in the morning before I do, he can haul himself up and look out the window.

When Miss O'Connor told us at school about the dangers of lead paint, I nearly choked. I could hardly wait to get home and check up on that window sill. It was all banged up, but the chips seemed tight, so that was a relief. I covered the sill up with contact paper, and I try not to worry about it. If you worry about everything that can go wrong, you'll never have any peace.

I do worry about the endangered species. That is kind of stupid because I can't do much about them, but still I do worry. Even about spotted owls and the little fish called snail darters. I'm afraid that when I grow up there won't be any animals left except people and the ones we eat.

Here's what I think. Even bugs have as much right to live as people. People say you have to value people more than any other living thing, but I don't believe that. I'm sorry, but I just don't. There are a lot of people who aren't worth anything. They just break things up. If I had to choose between saving those people and a single, solitary spotted owl, I would not hesitate. People are much more likely to be worthless than any other animal. I know that is disloyal to say, but it's the truth, and we might as well face it.

Stoppard sleeps on the fold-out couch in the living room. Lots of people sleep on fold-out couches, so I don't think there can be anything wrong with that. He is six. If we're watching a programme on television that he doesn't like, he thinks he can change the channel without majority rule because the couch is his bed. If he's cross he says get off my bed. I made a rule that it isn't his bed until it's unfolded, but after that he can say what we watch. If he doesn't want to watch anything, then he goes and gets in my bed. I don't mind that. I do have to do one thing, and that is catch him before he goes tight asleep and stand him up in front of the pot. Otherwise he will pee in the bed nine times out of ten. You only have to wake up peed on once before you learn to be careful.

My mom has her own room. The bathroom is right next to it, and everything works in there except the hot water faucet in the sink. You can turn it in any direction as many times as you like, and it doesn't do anything. But there is another faucet underneath the sink right next to the wall. It's a little faucet, and if you turn it you can make the hot water stop and go.

The other room in our apartment is the kitchen. It is a big room, and there is a stove and a refrigerator. There is also room for a table and chairs by the back door, so all in all you can see that we're pretty well equipped. We are going to get a dinette set as soon as we find one we like. They have dinette sets for $179.99 plus tax at Wal-Mart, but Mom doesn't like the style. She says she would rather do without than buy something that doesn't appeal to her. We were walking by Rare Earths the other day where they sell antique Fifties furniture. Mom stopped and said oh my god. It turned out that in the window they had a dinette set that was the exact same as the one my mom grew up with in Hibbing. It was old-fashioned and made out of chrome and formica. There were two chairs in the window and another two inside the store. The seats had a pattern done in red marbleized plastic. The whole set was in gorgeous shape, and we went in to see how much it cost.

The owner had a big, grey moustache. He said the set was four hundred dollars.

Mom almost fell down. Four hundred dollars!

Yes. It's an antique. A collector's item.

Mom told him it was exactly like the table her mother had in Hibbing, Minnesota, where she grew up.

They threw it out, she said. They threw it out when I graduated from high school and bought this fake country oak thing. It broke my heart.

The man told her that people often don't realize the value of the things in their basements. He had his own sad story, about how he'd thrown out an old-fashioned bicycle when he was young because he was moving to a new apartment and didn't want to be bothered.

He could tell Mom really wanted that table, and so he said he'd let it go for three fifty if she could swing it.

She laughed. I couldn't swing a dead cat, she said.

Outside the store she's all smiles. Let's go down to Sweet Tooth and get a cone, she says.

18

I have to remind her we are going to pick up Tyler at day care. And we can't afford it.

Oh that's right, she says and laughs some more. We walk down the street holding hands. After a minute she is squeezing my fingers so tight I can hardly stand it. Her eyes are all squinched up to keep back the tears.

This isn't the way it was supposed to be, she says.

She must have really wanted that dinette set.

Miss Paschonelle says there is a possibility that the boys and me might be put in care with Dr and Mrs Hoeksema in Hibbing. I don't think that is a good idea. I will now explain why.

They are too old to raise another family. They have worked hard all their lives and earned a peaceful retirement.

This is an exact quote from Mrs Hoeksema.

When Mom was a junior at the University of Minnesota in Minneapolis, she and her family had a break-up. It started because she wanted to go to English class, but these people wouldn't let her in the building. They were Native Americans holding a protest. The way they protested was to hold the doors and not let anyone in the building.

Mom said I don't see what this has to do with English literature.

This man said I don't see what English literature has to do with anything.

His name was Charles Taylor and he was a Native American. He and Mom hit it off, and they moved in together into an apartment near Dinkytown, and that was where I was born.

I don't remember that apartment, but Mom said it had belonged to drug addicts. They had painted the doors chocolate brown and purple, and it was very dirty. One day she found me playing with an old condom that I had found under the linoleum.

That's it, she says. That is absolutely it.

Charles Taylor went to work in construction in Houston, and Mom and me moved to the second floor in 1050 13th Ave S.E.

When you went in the door you were in the kitchen. Then you went up two steps and you were in the living room. Then you went through a door and that was the bedroom, and that was the whole apartment. The bathroom was in the hall, but we didn't have to share it because the other apartment on the second floor was jammed with furniture that the landlord left there when he moved to Arizona. The wallpaper on the stairs was made out of sandpaper and painted green. If you fell down the stairs, it took your skin off. This happened to me more than once.

Downstairs was Agnes Beauchamp. She was in the Licensed Practical Nurse programme at the U. If you jumped down the steps between the living room and the kitchen, she would come upstairs and complain, but in a nice way. She worked nights and had to sleep during the days. This was all right with me. When I came home from school in the afternoon, I would often as not have breakfast with Agnes. Breakfast at two o'clock in the afternoon! I liked that. When Charles Taylor came back from Houston, he'd go out to Dunkin Donuts and get a dozen assorted doughnuts for the three of us.

But that was later.

Agnes had a ratty bathrobe and a flannel nightie

underneath. If you stood against her and stuck your nose close, you could smell the bathrobe. It smelled like Agnes, as if it had soaked some of her up. Some people would say that it was too strong, but I liked the smell of her. I think how a person smells is important. If I meet someone new, I look for a chance to see what they smell like. I can't like a person if they don't have the right smell.

We also had a big back porch with glass windows up and down. It was unheated however. In the winter we stuck our garbage out there so we wouldn't have to carry it down the stairs. It got frozen and didn't have an odour.

In the back yard was a little shed that was stuffed with junk, and nobody went into it. Once when I took the garbage out to the porch, I saw a big bird come out of the little shed and attack a small white dog. It got it with its beak and shook it until the neck snapped. You could see blood on the fur. The bird dragged it back into the shed and wasn't seen again.

It wasn't a bird that flies. It walked. It had little round wings and a fluffy tail. Later I saw a picture of it in a book and learned that it is called the Flightless Dodo Bird. I told the teacher that we had one in our shed, and she just laughed and said it was extinct. The whole class laughed at me and didn't even check it out. I said you wouldn't laugh so much if it got one of you, but I didn't really want that to happen. I'm glad to say I never saw another bird like that, so maybe they are extinct now the way that teacher said.

Charles Taylor came for Christmas and we went outside and shovelled the driveway. When it was all shovelled, there were big banks of snow on both sides. They were up to my chest. Charles Taylor picked me up and threw me up in the air so I came down crashing in the snow. It didn't hurt because the snow was so deep. It was too deep to walk in, so Charles Taylor pulled me out. My jacket got over my head and my shirt got untucked.

What's this, he said, and put his cold mitten on my bare belly.

I was laughing and screaming. Mom came out of the house and stood on the porch in her nightie with her hands folded under her chest. What are you two doing? she said.

We made a run at her and she jumped back in the house with her nightie flapping.

You're crazy, she says. Both of you.

That is one memory I have of him.

He didn't like the air in the apartment. He said it couldn't circulate. Before the landlord went to Arizona, he hired some men to put up the storm windows. The hooks were broken, so they just nailed them down. Mom tried to explain to Charles Taylor that there was nothing they could do.

I can't breathe in here, he said.

I'm sorry, but we can't open the window. It's nailed shut. That's what I'm trying to tell you.

Charles Taylor said I'll open the window. He pushed up the inside sash and threw a can of tuna fish through the storm.

Now it's open, he said.

He said he was going to stay a while and got a job trimming trees for a landscape company. He was the one they sent up to the top where no one else would go. He had a chainsaw on a rope, and he walked around in the top of the tree like he was on the sidewalk.

Mom went back to school so she could get her degree in English literature. She was going to be a high school teacher. She said she was going to Eau Claire with her friend Esther to see an art show. She said don't wait up because we might stay over.

Charles Taylor woke me up. He got me out of bed and said you sit here. I sat on the couch in the dark while he went around on tiptoe and peeked out the windows.

He came back and sat down beside me.

He says your mom didn't go to Eau Claire with Esther. She didn't?

No. She went to the airport motel with Peter Hobbs. At this moment she's fucking Peter Hobbs at the airport.

Oh, I said.

Do you know what fucking is?

Yes.

That's when the man sticks his dinkus up your pussy. That's what Peter Hobbs is doing. He's sticking his dinkus up your mama's pussy. You think about that.

The next morning we had French toast for breakfast and Charles Taylor took me to work with him instead of first grade.

He took me up in the tree with him. We had ropes on. They went over a limb and down to the men watching. Forget about the ropes, Charles Taylor said, and just pretend that this is where you belong. This is your natural environment. So I walked around in the top of the tree with him and wasn't at all afraid. He had a little curved saw, and I held it for him when he wasn't using it. I stood on a little limb not holding on to anything and looked down at the men with their mouths open. I remember it very clearly.

Mom said this couldn't possibly have happened. Mr

Pierce was the crew boss and he wouldn't have let Charles Taylor take me up in a tree like that.

How would you know? I say. You weren't there. I know where you were. You were out at the airport, letting Peter Hobbs stick his thing in you.

Mom kicked Charles Taylor out after that, and I didn't see him again. He died of carbon monoxide poisoning about a month later. He and two of his friends had parked the pick-up underneath the Franklin Ave bridge and were drinking Ripple. They kept the motor running to stay warm and it poisoned the air. There was a hole in the back window but Charles Taylor had sealed it up with duct tape, so they weren't to be saved by that.

The police came to our house because that was the address on his driver's licence. It was early morning and I had my school clothes on. Mom was in bed because she was pregnant with Stoppard at the time.

Agnes Beauchamp brought the police upstairs and knocked on our door. She was in her practical nurse's uniform and had her hand over her mouth.

Oh, Linda, she says and starts bawling.

There were two policemen standing behind her. I thought she was under arrest, and I ran and hid in Mom's closet. I've always been ashamed of that reaction. My first impulse wasn't to try to help her but to run and hide.

I could hear people shouting and crying, Agnes most of all, but I didn't come out. I jammed the sleeve of one of Mom's old jackets into my mouth and didn't budge.

When they all went away, I came out of the closet. Mom was gone too. I thought it was possible that she'd been arrested as well, but I wasn't sure. I got my own breakfast and went to school, just like always. I thought that was the best plan. I was afraid that if I acted out of the ordinary I would get picked up by the FBI.

The crossing guard held up her hand and said stop, and I nearly fainted. But it was only for a car turning right.

I don't know how I got through the morning, but I did. Just before lunch, Mrs James, the principal's secretary, hauls me out of class, and Mom's standing in the hall with Peter Hobbs and her hands in her pockets.

Your father's dead, she says.

Who?

Your father. Charles Taylor. It was an auto accident. He killed himself, she said.

I didn't know what I was supposed to do then. Go back to class or what.

Take it easy, Sandra, Peter says to Mom. He was a college boy at that time. He had short red hair and freckles.

Take what easy? Mom snaps. Somebody's got to tell her.

She looks at me.

Your dad's dead. You understand me? She grabs my arm and gives me a shake. Don't you understand? Don't you understand anything?

I started to cry then, and everybody was relieved to get a reaction.

It's the shock, Mrs James said.

Later Mom tells me more exactly what happened. About the carbon monoxide and the bottles of Ripple.

There were nine empty bottles on the floor of that

pick-up, she says. She's sitting cross-legged on the bed with her belly in her lap and rocking back and forth.

That's three apiece. Those bastards were drunk out of their minds.

You know that hole in the back window? I begged him to get that fixed, but he couldn't be bothered. You know what that jerk did? He covered the whole thing up with duct tape. He wouldn't do it for me. But he'd do it for no reason. He'd do it so he could kill himself.

After Charles Taylor killed himself, Mom and Peter Hobbs made all kinds of plans. He brought Chinese take-out for supper, and they sat on her bed and talked. She pushed her trousers down so her bare belly stuck up, and Peter rubbed it with Vitamin E so she wouldn't get stretch marks. I did that too, and sometimes I could feel Stoppard moving around inside.

One plan was that they would buy a large sailboat and live on it in the Caribbean. Peter said they could make a living taking rich people on cruises. He had crewed once on an America's Cup boat and knew all about sailing.

That was one plan.

Another was that they would buy this old schoolhouse out in the country, and Mom could be a potter, and Peter would make handmade canoes.

It was all hot air.

I don't know whether or not Mom and Peter knew it was just hot air. Sometimes they had serious fights about some dumb plan to smuggle dope or start a nursery. Mom wanted to skip electricity in the schoolhouse they were going to buy in the country, and Peter all but said it was a stupid idea. They had a huge fight, and Mom had to back down.

I got it into my head that I wanted to see Peter's dinkus. Miss Paschonelle says it was because of what Charles Taylor had told me about his sticking Mom with it, but I can't say that I feel that's the right explanation. My main interest was to see if it had freckles like his face.

I asked him if he would show it to me, and he laughed the question off and said I was too little.

One day Mom was at the hospital class. That was where she learned how to breathe when she was having a baby. He said I could see his dick now if I wanted.

All right, I said.

He took me in the bedroom and threw me on the bed. Then he pulled the window shade. He sat down next to me and took his dick out of his pants. I'd never seen anything like it before. It was stretchy and brown and I thought it was a fake. I thought he was joking me and it was just something he'd just stuck in his pants when he was standing by the window.

He said I could pull on it if I wanted, but I said no, I don't want to.

He said now we'll have a look at you.

He took my trousers down and held my legs up so he could see. Then he felt me with his finger. He pushed it up me and felt my belly button from the inside.

Do you like that? he says.

Yes, I said.

Well, you shouldn't, he says. You're not supposed to let people touch you. You understand? From now on. I just wanted to see if you knew any better.

He wiped his hands on his hanky and then he went

away. I lay for a long time on the bed with my trousers around my ankles. I didn't know if I was supposed to pull them up or wait until he came back. I didn't want to do anything wrong.

He never did come back, though, so finally I must have pulled them up myself.

I don't remember, really.

I didn't tell Mom. Miss Paschonelle wanted to know if he warned me not to, but that wasn't necessary. I knew better on my own.

Just before Stoppard was due to be born, Mr and Mrs Hobbs showed up. They were from Winnetka. Mrs Hobbs was young and pretty. She was red-haired like Peter, and her skin was so thin you could see veins through it. When I tried to get close, it made her nervous. She laughed it off at first, but then she says Linda, I want you to sit in that chair over there, and don't you move a muscle.

Peter takes me over and plops me in that cold chair. He sits me down so hard it hurts.

They had a talk about what was to be done.

Mom said Peter had to marry her because he was Stoppard's daddy.

Mrs Hobbs hops in and says we don't know that. We don't know that Peter's the father. You were married to another man, weren't you?

Mr Hobbs says please, Grace. Let me handle this.

I just want to know, says Mrs Hobbs. That's reasonable, isn't it? I mean, I assume she was having sex with the man who died.

Mr Hobbs got her shut up finally. Then he explained

that while they felt sorry for Mom, they couldn't really allow Peter to get married at this time. He was very young. He had his education to finish. When he was out of law school, then he could marry anybody he wanted, but not yet.

How old is she, anyway? says Mrs Hobbs. That little girl must be six or seven. Sandra must be ten years older than Peter.

Mom asked Peter if he was going to let them talk to her that way, and he got very red in the face. But it was plain he wasn't going to defy his parents.

He told Mom she had to be reasonable. He was going to marry her, but they had to wait. All of those plans they'd talked about were just daydreams. That wasn't being realistic.

I knew that, Mom said. I knew that right from the start.

They made some sort of arrangement. I forget what. Mr and Mrs Hobbs were going to help Mom with the expenses of Stoppard getting born, and then they'd see. They didn't even say Peter couldn't see Mom. Mr Hobbs just wanted them both to be reasonable and take things slowly. There was no need to be reckless with either of their futures.

I think if Mrs Hobbs had had her way and said all she was thinking, then there would have been a big fight, and Mom and Peter would have run off and got married. But Mr Hobbs put the brakes on his wife and kept talking about how we had to be reasonable and look after the interests of not only Peter and Mom but the child too.

After that, Mom didn't have a hope. Peter came over

a few more times, but since his father had worked out everything about the future, they didn't have anything to talk about. They could just fight about his mother. They broke up about two weeks after Stoppard was born. That was the last I ever saw of him. I was sorry when he left, because he was pretty nice most of the time. He took me to the Como Zoo once. That was one nice memory I have of him.

After Peter stopped coming, his father called up and said they were no longer persuaded that Stoppard was their grandchild and they didn't feel they could afford to give Mom any more support.

Mom said she was going to sue, but Mr Hobbs stayed calm. He said that was fine. He thought it was a matter best decided by the courts.

Mr Hobbs gave Mom some cash settlement, but it wasn't much. He knew Mom was all talk and wouldn't do anything.

Things reached a low point after that. Mom had already dropped out of school, and when the money that Mr Hobbs gave her ran out, we were in bad shape. Mom just sat around in her bathrobe and smoked cigarettes. She wasn't even up to taking care of Stoppard, really. She made a show when the nurse from the hospital came round, and got dressed and cleaned up a bit, but otherwise she was clinically depressed.

I stopped going to school. I didn't want to go and nobody made me. I stood at the front window and watched the other kids going by on their way to second grade. A girl named Mary O'Brian twirled around and fell down in the snow in our front yard. She made a snow angel on our snow without even asking. As soon as she was gone, I went out and stomped it up.

I had to take care of Stoppard too, which is partly why we're so bonded. As he got older it was pretty clear that Peter was his daddy just like Mom always said. He has carroty hair and freckles, but I don't hold that against him.

I fried eggs for supper because that was what I knew how to do. I liked to watch the egg whites turn cloudy, and I would test the yolk with my finger to see if it was hard enough. When it was just right I would put it on a piece of toast and eat it. One time I found a piece of blood in the egg and I showed it to Mom. She scratched it out with her fingernail and smeared it on the plate.

I now understand True Peace and how to obtain it, she said.

She gave me the chills because True Peace didn't have anything to do with that egg.

She said all you have to do is Cease Striving. If you do that, you will feel complete peace.

I say if you do that you will starve to death in no time.

It was lucky Mom stocked up a big supply of baby food and formula before she ceased striving, or Stoppard would have been in real trouble. When I was really hungry I would sometimes eat his stuff.

That is another thing I'm ashamed of, but nothing bad came of it, because things were straightened out before he was actually deprived.

What happened is that I tried to trade a desk light at the 7-Eleven for some TV dinners. It was a teenager that was waiting on me, and he just laughed in my face. But a lady heard me talking to him, and she asked me where I got the desk light. I didn't want to talk to her, but she bugged me until I told her I got it off the desk at home.

Does your mother know what you're doing? she says.

I shut up then, but she wouldn't let the matter drop. I forget her name, but she was a law student at the U. If I need a lawyer in this case, I think I will look her up. Ha ha.

She took me home and knocked on the door.

I didn't tell her that I was on the second floor, and so she knocked on Agnes's door. When Agnes opens up, she doesn't know what's happening, but then the lady explains what she saw.

I'm very concerned, she says.

She and Agnes go upstairs and find Mom spaced out in bed and Stoppard in a diaper that I dried out over the heat vent and then used again. And no food in the cupboard.

I'll take over from here, Agnes says.

She takes Stoppard and me downstairs and feeds us lunch. Then she goes to the store and buys some diapers and other necessaries with her own money. When we get home she goes up to have a talk with Mom.

She tells Mom she's going to call Hibbing.

If you do that I'll never speak to you again, Mom says, but Agnes says she's going to do it anyway.

Mom says you were screwing Charles Taylor, weren't you? You let him nail you to the wall every chance you got. He always liked girls without any tits. Well, I hope you enjoyed it because now he's dead and you can just sit on your finger for the rest of your life.

Well, thank you, Sandra, says Agnes. You're making this real easy for me.

She turns around and walks out the door.

Where are you going? I say.

I'm going to call your grandparents, she says.

I didn't even know I had grandparents.

Who are they? I shout down the stairs.

Dr and Mrs Chester Hoeksema of Hibbing, Minnesota, she shouts back.

Dr and Mrs Chester Hoeksema of Hibbing, Minnesota! They sounded big and solid. I could see them already in my mind's eye. The doctor fat and moving slow and his wife in a hat with cherries on it.

I flew back into Mom's room.

I said Agnes is going to call your mom and dad. I already know their names. They're Dr and Mrs Chester Hoeksema of Hibbing, Minnesota. They'll probably come over here and take charge.

Mom gives me a long look.

Don't get your hopes up, she says.

But she was wrong about the Hoeksemas. We were going to be saved, temporarily at least.

3

Mom said when your granddad comes, you call him Dr Hoeksema, you understand? You say yes sir no sir.

She got a suitcase down from the shelf in the closet and opened it up. It had clothes inside I hadn't seen before.

I said whose are those?

These are mine, she says. These are my college clothes. She runs her fingers over the stuff and starts to cry.

I threw the shoes away, she says. They were such beautiful shoes and I threw them away.

That's OK, because at least she is out of bed.

I stood myself at the front window so I'd be the first to see him when he arrived.

What kind of car does he drive? I say.

Who?

Dr Hoeksema.

I don't know. He always bought Buicks. What are you doing?

Watching to see him.

Well he's not coming today. You thought he was coming today? He's not coming until Friday. Hibbing's a long way from here.

How far?

A million miles.

*

Before we could do anything else, all the garbage that was frozen on the back porch had to be carried down and piled around the trash can next to Agnes's back door. I did that.

Mom borrowed twenty-five dollars and went to Dinkytown to get her hair cut. She took one of her college suits with her on a hanger to get pressed.

Agnes came upstairs while she was gone, and we cleaned the place up.

She found an old shirt of Charles Taylor's and sat down on the bed with her face in it.

She said I really loved your dad. He had his problems, but he was a good man. She started to cry and put her arms around me. I'm going to miss you, she said.

I stood stiff. Over her shoulder I could see Mom was back and I didn't want her to see me hugging somebody else. She was standing in the door waiting for Agnes to stop going on about Charles Taylor.

Well, well, she says. She had on the suit. It had tight sleeves and a short skirt. She looked like a million dollars.

I wrote a bad cheque on these shoes, she tells Agnes. She holds up a foot for us to see. I thought you might give me the money to cover it.

All right.

Let's be explicit. I thought you might give me the money because you screwed Charles Taylor until his dick fell off.

I said I would.

Good. I got something out of this marriage.

She hooks her hair back behind her ears.

Look at my hands, she says. I'm shaking.

We went downstairs to have one last cigarette with Agnes in her apartment.

Mom says if Daddy finds out I was smoking when I was pregnant, I won't hear the end of it.

You think you can quit?

Yes. I'm not even enjoying this cigarette.

She looks around the room.

Sometimes this part of my life all seems like a bad dream, she says.

Well. It's over now.

I want to start over. That's what I want. You know my dad wanted me to go to medical school? I was smart enough. But I was going to be a songwriter. I may even have thought I'd be some kind of pop star. It's possible. I was that naive.

It's because of your looks. It's hard for a girl to be so attractive.

You know that's true? You don't realize how vulnerable you are. That's the main thing.

We all make mistakes.

We sure do.

Mom looks at me and wrinkles up her nose.

Did Stoppard fill his pants? What'd you bring him down here for? she says.

I take Stoppard upstairs and change his pants, and then we stand by the window. A big car pulls up in the snow, and a man gets out and looks up and down the street. He's hunched and got on a red and black checked Mackinaw. He is not fat like I imagined, but still I know who it is.

That's him, I tell Stoppard. That's your granddad.

Dr Hoeksema loaded us up that afternoon.

He said we're not taking any more than we can get in the back, so make up your mind.

That's all right, Mom says. I don't want any of it.

If this is going to work, you have to put that part of your life behind you.

I know, I know, Mom says, but she cries all the way to Hibbing.

Look at my eyes, she says. I'm a mess.

When we got to Hibbing, Mrs Hoeksema came out of a flat house all covered with snow and looked in the back seat at me. She was a big woman with a little head all covered with yellow curls.

Mom says give your grandma a big hug, but the old lady holds me off so she can check me over.

What a nice complexion, she says. She'll never need a suntan.

Yes, says Mom. She never has anything wrong with her skin. It's always nice and smooth.

Lots of oil in it. Yes, well, she'll have to look out for pimples later. That oily skin . . . She must take after her daddy's family.

Yes, I suppose she does.

Yes . . .

She took to Stoppard right away.

Look at this, Mother, Mom says. She takes off Stoppard's baby hat. You can see his hairs coming in fine and reddish blond behind the black fur he was born with.

Mrs Hoeksema says why he hardly looks Indian at all. I never saw an Indian baby with red hair.

Oh sure, says Mom. I saw one in the National Geographic. It's unusual, but it happens.

Well, isn't that something. Look at his scalp! Mrs Hoeksema says. It's all scaly. What have you been using on his head?

I tried everything. I just don't know what to do.

You haven't been using Johnson's, have you. You've been using some store-brand baby shampoo.

I don't know. Maybe.

They go in the bathroom and give Stoppard a bath right off. When they dress him on the bed, Mrs Hoeksema lifts up his legs and examines his equipment.

Goodness, she says.

What's the matter?

Nothing. Your brother wasn't quite like that.

Bobby was circumcised. I decided not to do that with Stoppard.

You think that's a good idea? You don't want infections. It's harder to keep it clean this way. Did the doctor explain that to you?

Yes, he said there wasn't any reason, really, to have it done.

They handle themselves more if it's like this. I suppose you know that.

That's superstition. They handle themselves all the time anyway.

Later I asked Mom what happened to her brother, and she said they cut some of the skin off his penis when he was a baby. She said it was a minor operation and didn't amount to much.

Is he around here? I say. I thought I might ask to see his dick and compare it to Stoppard's.

No, Mom says. He lives in Duluth.

In Hibbing the food was good, but it was nearly all soft. We had salmon loaf for supper and tapioca for dessert.

Dr Hoeksema ate celery to help his digestion.

38

Mom says you know what? I think Linda's eyes are just like Aunt Ruth's.

I sit up and let everybody see my eyes.

Mrs Hoeksema gives me a look.

Ruth's eyes are green, she says.

Yes, I know. That's what I mean. Linda's eyes remind me of hers.

I don't know why. Linda's eyes are tan coloured. Not green.

They're a little green.

Have it your own way.

They're hazel, says Mom and starts to cry.

Dr Hoeksema tries to calm everybody down. They're very unusual eyes, he says. Amber I would say.

After supper I sit on his lap and he shows me the album.

When Mom was in high school she was a cheerleader and one of the homecoming queen's maids of honour. She would have been homecoming queen, but they had to give the crown to a girl who had polio.

That's Carol Bloomberg. There she is, says Dr Hoeksema.

He points to a girl in the book. She's in a blue dress and holding on to a boy. She's got metal canes with hooks for her elbows. They are all but covered up by her skirt, but they are there if you know where to look.

Dr Hoeksema says she was the last girl in Hibbing to have polio. There was no excuse really. They already had the vaccine. Her parents were careless about health matters. They were the Jews who ran the clothing store on Main Street. That polio was the only reason she got the crown.

Now that isn't fair, Mom says. Carol Bloomberg was really popular and she deserved it.

Mrs Hoeksema was already knitting a sweater for Stoppard. Blue for a boy.

Maybe you're right after all, she says. Carol is a lawyer now in St Paul and is married to the man that has the largest Pontiac dealership in the Midwest.

Mom says what's that supposed to mean?

It doesn't mean anything. I was just agreeing with you.

Mom's bottom lip comes out. I go over to stroke her up, but she pushes me away.

What are you leaning on me for? she says.

She complains about me to Mrs Hoeksema.

She's always holding on to me, she says. Sometimes I can't get my breath.

Mrs Hoeksema goes tsk tsk. She's the clingy type, she says. You see that sometimes.

Mom turns me around and slaps my bottom.

Make yourself useful and go see if Stoppard kicked off his covers, she says.

In Hibbing we had a whole house. It was in the country. There was a two-car garage but only one car. Dr Hoeksema kept his bass boat on its trailer on the other side. There was also a small tractor. I hoped I could ride that and mow the grass when spring came, but Dr Hoeksema said no. He wanted to keep the mowing for himself.

They stuck me in a room alone. That was the first time I'd had my own room, and I didn't understand that it was a good thing. I wanted to sleep with Mom and Stoppard in the guest room.

Mrs Hoeksema says no, that's unhealthy.

She marches me down the narrow stairs.

This is your room for the time being, she says. Now no back talk.

She leaned over and flicked my ear with her finger. She did that every chance she got when nobody was looking.

The room was in the basement, but that's not as bad as it sounds. The house was on a hill, and the basement had windows and a door in the back. You wouldn't even know it was a basement from that angle. From my window you could see across the valley, and it was a pleasant view. The big problem was that it wasn't really my room. It was Robert Hoeksema's room.

He was the one who had part of his dink cut off.

Nothing in his room was to be disturbed. There were pictures of Wonder Woman on the wall and one of Jane Fonda as Barbarella. There were also a bunch of model aeroplanes and an electric guitar. If you lifted up the lid on his desk, there was a shallow place where he kept a couple of Playboys dated long ago. One featured Linda Lovelace who had a scar on her stomach and no hair. I looked at those sometimes and had bad thoughts. You will find those in Miss Paschonelle's report, so there is no need to go into them here.

I didn't tell her about one other thing I did. I also broke one of his model aeroplanes on purpose. It was made out of balsa wood and covered with tissue paper. There was a little hole in the paper on one wing, and I started poking at it with a paper clip that I had unbent. Not all at once, but over about a week. I would sit in school and think about the damage I was doing, and I could hardly wait to get home to do some more. At the same time I felt sick about it. The hole got bigger and bigger, and then one Saturday when no one was around,

I broke the whole thing. I held it on my lap under the table and crushed it up slowly. I felt choked while I was doing it, but I couldn't stop myself. I was afraid it would be found if I threw it out, so I hid it in the space behind the washing machine.

Robert showed up at Easter. I looked at his pants where his thing was supposed to be, but didn't see anything wrong. I realized that I wasn't going to be able to ask him to show it to me because it turned out he was a grown-up. He had a wife and two little girls of his own. They had skimpy blonde hair. The littlest one was blue around the edges. His wife brought a casserole made out of sweet potatoes and marshmallows.

I was afraid he was going to notice that one of his aeroplanes was missing and have a fit. But nothing like that happened. He was nice to me right from the start. He looked in the room and said why don't you clear out some of this junk?

Mrs Hoeksema said she wanted to keep that room just as it was when he was in high school.

He said it's not a museum, Mother, and threw out a bunch of old stuff including the posters. He didn't make me move out. He and his family spent the night in the rec room. When they got up they ate Eggos for breakfast and then drove back to Duluth.

When he went away the Playboys were gone too, and I was both glad I wouldn't be tempted any more but sad too.

Mrs Hoeksema held it against me that the posters got destroyed. She probably didn't know about the Playboys.

She said that if it wasn't for me, then everything could go back just as it was. They would all take a vacation trip to Hawaii, and include Stoppard and the two little girls.

She suggested I run away, but I wouldn't do it just to please her.

Miss Paschonelle wonders if my memory wasn't playing a trick at this point, but it's all true. We were in the laundry room washing out an empty Downy fabric softener bottle at the time.

She says you ever think about going to see your other grandmother?

What other grandmother?

Your Indian one. You'd fit right in there. With your own kind of people. Maybe you should run away next time you get sulky, and go stay with her. You ever think of that?

That's what she said.

I went back to school. I rode a school bus that stopped at the mailbox in front. I made a friend right away. Her name was Sara Anderson, and I went over to her house to play every chance I could.

Her mother didn't work. She cleaned up the kitchen after breakfast and called her friends on the telephone. She kept a close eye on me and used to give me little lessons in manners.

Linda? What do you do when a grown-up comes in the room?

(You stand up.)

Linda? What do you say?

(Good afternoon, Mrs Anderson.)

She saw me scratching my feet and put athlete's foot powder between my toes and gave me a clean pair of Sara's socks. I started to love her then, but she told Sara's dad that she wished I wasn't around all the time. She was afraid I was a bad influence.

I felt real inadequate after that.

I tried to break up with Sara for a while, but I couldn't do it. I liked her too much. So I still went over to her house and felt worse than ever.

She had a big brother whose name was Johnny Anderson. He had his own room, and we went in there and looked in his drawers when he wasn't home. His top drawer was full of white socks, and I stole one when no one was looking. I kept it in the secret drawer of Robert's desk where the Playboys used to be. I kept Sara's socks in there too. The ones I wore home with the powder inside. Sometimes I sat in Robert Hoeksema's room and pretended that Johnny Anderson was my big brother and on his way home from school. When he comes in, he finds me there messing with his socks.

You need a whipping, he says. He makes me lie on my stomach and spanks me good.

You can see I had a crush on Sara's brother. But he didn't even know I was alive.

Mom came home from the Red Owl. She had a job there as a cashier.

Guess who I saw today, she says.

Who?

Mr Bloomberg! Carol Bloomberg's daddy. His wife died. Did you know that?

Mrs Hoeksema tries to remember. She was making Twenty-four Hour Salad, and I had to peel the grapes.

I did see that somewhere, she says. I thought they moved to Florida and she died there.

Yes, in St Petersburg. He just came back to see to

some real estate. I asked how Carol was and he said she was having her third child. She had to stay in bed for six months because of the polio.

Mrs Hoeksema said that defective people shouldn't be allowed to have children. She was also hot on juvenile crime. She knew of a way to keep all of those girls in the ghetto from getting pregnant, but it wasn't fit for a child's ears.

Mr Bloomberg came over and joined Dr Hoeksema on the screened-in porch. Dr Hoeksema was having his evening Manhattan, and so he had to ask Mr Bloomberg if he wanted one too.

Mr Bloomberg said he wouldn't say no. He said he was going back to Florida as soon as his business was straightened out.

When will that be?

Soon.

It turned out that he had come over to invite Mom to the movies. While she went to get dressed, he told Dr Hoeksema about a good investment. Nucor Steel.

When he and Mom were gone, the Doctor said well what in the Sam Hill? That was the most awkward ten minutes of my entire life. What is that girl up to, anyway? That man is older than I am.

In school Sara had the idea that we would switch clothes and see what happened, and so we did. We were about the same size.

We had a man teacher. His name was Mr Keller and he didn't even notice. Everybody in the class knew, but he didn't.

He says that's a pretty sweater you have on today, Linda, and the class just about breaks up.

After that, switching clothes became sort of a craze. Just the girls did it and not the boys.

Once I switched with three girls in a single day. Mr Keller knew that something funny was happening, but he couldn't figure out what.

Usually we got all switched back by the end of the day, but sometimes we didn't, and it wasn't long before some of the mothers found out.

One of them complained, and the principal sent home a note with all the girls. He hoped the parents would help the school put an end to this unladylike fad.

Mom says did you do this stuff?

Yes.

Well. Don't do it any more.

All right.

I went out to sit in a beech tree out back. There were good branches to sit on.

Mom calls me to come in the house again.

Wait a minute, she says. Who'd you do this with?

Sara.

Anybody else?

No.

All right. Just don't do it any more. Somebody went to the school and had a fit.

That was Mrs Miller.

Cassandra Miller came home with Susan Jenkins's underwear on her. Her mother found out because there was a name tag inside.

I never heard of such a thing. You weren't supposed to switch underwear, but just your outside clothes.

Cassandra couldn't even get her own underpants back

because Susan buried them somewhere in the woods when the storm burst.

A woman came to the school. She was dressed in powder blue. I saw her talking to the principal in the hall, and she had a bungee cord in her hand.

She lived in a room without any windows. That was so no one could see what happened there. Someone came and got you out of class and you went to the windowless room.

Susan Jenkins came out crying in front of me. She ran down the hall in jerky little steps like she had to go pee. Her skirt flipped up and I could see her pants. I thought she'd got a whipping and that was what the lady was there for. To whip us with the bungee cord.

The lady was waiting for me. She had her hands folded. She told me her name but I forget. She asked me about home and what I thought of the weather in Hibbing, and then we got down to business.

Where did you and your friends do the switching?

In the Girls' Room.

You didn't do it in the classroom?

That would be a dumb idea with the boys there, but she didn't seem to understand that.

You remember that time when you stayed after to rehearse for the spring assembly?

Yes.

There were seven of you, weren't there?

She rattled off a list of names, and it sounded OK to me.

Did you do any switching then?

No.

Did any of the other girls?

No, I don't think so.

Well. Didn't someone suggest playing a game of some kind? Maybe a dress-up game? Where you take off your clothes?

She had a bee in her bonnet about taking off your clothes.

She says let's approach this from a different angle. You remember that day of the rehearsal? she starts off.

Yes.

When you took off your clothes? Did anybody touch you in a way you didn't like?

No.

Well, who touched you? Did Mr Keller touch you?

No, he didn't.

Well, who did? You don't have to worry, Linda. You don't have to be afraid. Did anyone touch you?

When we did the flower dance.

The what?

The flower dance.

That's interesting. Was this something Mr Keller told you to do?

Yes.

Was he the one who touched you?

No, I don't think so.

Who touched you?

Sara did. We had the dance.

I see. Did somebody tell Sara to touch you?

It was the dance.

I see. Did Mr Keller tell Sara to touch you?

Yes.

She writes that down, and I didn't get whipped.

I went over to Sara's house, and her mom wouldn't let me in.

You go home to your own house, Linda. You're not to come over here any more.

Why?

I think you know why, Linda. I would be ashamed if I were you. We tried to be nice to you, and this is what we get.

When I walked away, I could see Sara looking at me out the window. She had just her head. The rest of her had been put away somewhere. The head was on the window sill with the eyes open like a pumpkin. When her mom saw I was looking at it, she came and carried it away.

I did see Sara whole after that, but it was from a distance.

I went home and climbed the tree in the backyard. I decided I wouldn't go to school any more. I didn't want to spill my guts to the lady in powder blue any more. I decided I would just ask her to whip me instead.

Mom came out of the house looking for me.

She says you come down here. I've got something to discuss with you.

No. I tell her no, and she went back in the house.

When it started to get dark at night, she came out again.

Linda? You come down right now. Some things have happened that you and me have to talk about.

I say I didn't know switching clothes was wrong. It was just a joke.

I don't care about that. Mr Bloomberg and I are going to get married.

What?

Mr Bloomberg and I are going to get married. We're all going to Florida.

49

Me and Stoppard, too?

Yes, now will you come down here? I don't enjoy shouting my news up a tree.

I came down then. I will be packed and ready in ten minutes is what I told her.

Mrs Hoeksema was in the dining room with all the lights on. It was too bright in there to look at her.

She said I don't know why she can't marry somebody of her own race. Just once.

Dr Hoeksema said now Mother, we're all members of the human race. He was brighter than the woman, and saw he was going to get rid of us for good, or so he hoped.

Mrs Hoeksema didn't want to let Stoppard go. That was the problem.

She said why don't you leave the baby here? You'll have more fun.

Mom said you'd like that, wouldn't you, Mother? You've always liked Robert more than me. Well, you can't have Stoppard too.

Mr Bloomberg came in a big Cadillac. It was sapphire blue with white leather inside. I got in the back. He pressed a button and the top flew off.

Ready in the front? Ready in the back?

Yes, I told him. Yes, I'm ready.

We roared off into the night. Mom sat in the front with Stoppard on her lap. The wind whipped her hair up around her face until she put on a scarf. I leaned back and looked at the stars. There were more that night than I ever saw before.

4

When I told Mr Bloomberg I'd never been swimming, he couldn't believe it.

Never?

No. Not one time.

We got in the car and drove to a store in St Petersburg. It was a long dark place. An old lady in sunglasses waited on us. She looked me over and said she's an eight. She could tell at a glance what size I was. She picked out some swimming suits that I might like, and while I tried to make up my mind, she and Mr Bloomberg talked about skin cancer. She showed him a spot on her arm.

Is that precancerous? she said. It was bleeding for no apparent reason yesterday.

The old worry a lot about cancer. There is no cure.

I learned to swim in the pool behind Mr Bloomberg's house. It wasn't large. About nine metres long. That was big enough. I plunged in and did the dog paddle until I got my confidence. That was all the training I had, but now I swim well. I'm absolutely fearless.

Sometimes we went to the beach. Mom sat in the shade with Stoppard, but Mr Bloomberg and I walked up and down along the shore. I got a good tan right away.

We collected shells, but the big ones were all gone.

He told me the sea life was dying off because of the pollution.

No one notices, he says. You have to be old to notice.

He points at some ripples in the water.

That's a rip tide, he says.

A rip tide will carry you out to drown if you stepped in the wrong place. He knew of a case. An Olympic swimmer. He thought he didn't have anything to worry about because he was such a wonderful swimmer, but the tide got him and sucked him under.

Mr Bloomberg and I would go in up to our ankles. I could feel the water sucking the sand out from under my feet. If I was carried away, the people on land wouldn't be able to help. They would run down the beach crying.

Out on an island in the bay were some new flat houses with white roofs. Mr Bloomberg explained that these were all going to get swept away in the next hurricane.

Ours, too?

Yes.

When will that be?

Soon, he says. It's overdue.

We'll have plenty of warning, Mom says. We'll all evacuate if anything like that happens.

I said yes, but I don't think I believed her. What if it came while I was alone with Stoppard? I decided finally if that happened, I would take him and run down to the marina next to the Port O'Call Motel and hop in a boat. That was the best I could think of.

I saw other kids at the beach, but I was too shy to talk to them. I could hardly wait for school to start.

We stayed in Florida for three years, and the first two were really good ones. At school everything seemed to go right. I got satisfactory in everything. I was a chunk in Hibbing, but now I started to shoot up and look good.

Mr Bloomberg and I hit it off right from the start. I took an interest in the stock market, and he bought me some shares to look after. The first time they went down I was tempted to sell, but he explained that was a common mistake.

That investment is sound and is going to pick up, he says. Its decline in value is due to inflationary pressures. That doesn't have anything to do with the strength of the company. So hold on.

Sell high and buy low.

That sounds like common sense, but if you study the investment patterns of many ordinary investors, you'll see that they often do it just the other way around. They buy some stock because it's on a roll, and then they panic and sell when there's some readjustment.

Every morning he read the *Wall Street Journal* at breakfast and we made decisions for the day. He'd call his broker after I went to school. When I got home we could do whatever we wanted.

We'd go over to the Port O'Call for Happy Hour. I enjoyed that. The waiter would bring me a Coke with a cherry and an umbrella in it.

Mr Bloomberg's friends would come over to the table and sit down. Mr Fine and Mr Shirmir.

Mr Fine had a Zippo lighter. He put it on the table in front of him next to his cigarettes. It had a picture of a fouled anchor on it. Underneath was the name of a boat. USS *Tarpon*. That was a torpedo boat. Mr Fine had served on it in the Pacific. He never talked about his experiences.

Do you know what a fouled anchor is?

No, sir.

That's when the anchor is entangled in its own line. It won't hold if that happens.

That's bad?

It can be fatal.

Oh, wow, I said.

Mr Shirmir had a glass eye. He said he was going to take it out and put it in his martini.

No, I said. Don't do it.

Yes, I'm going to.

No, don't.

What will you give me not to?

A kiss, I said.

I knew how to behave without being told.

They asked my advice on stocks or bonds.

Mr Shirmir said he was thinking of buying some common stock in GM. What do you think, Linda?

Oh, I'd say, I don't think GM is a good investment. Not at the moment. Have you seen their debt? That last union contract is going to cost them a billion dollars.

Mr Shirmir sat back and grinned.

Think of that, he said. Just think of that.

I was Arthur's girl. That's what the old men called me. That was Mr Bloomberg's name. Arthur Bloomberg.

At night I stood in the bedroom door and watched him get ready for bed. He took off his shoes and socks first. Then he wiggled his toes.

Free at last, he said. Thank God Almighty, free at last.

When he took off his trousers you could see he had a fat leather strap over his underpants.

What's that? I said.

That is an appliance, he said.

A what? I thought an appliance was a refrigerator.

A truss, he said. A monument to restraint.

Mom gets in the way and pushes me out into the hall.

Why aren't you in bed? she says.

I knew Mom wasn't as happy as I was, but I blocked it out. I was happy myself. When I saw she needed some attention, I'd say no, I'm too busy.

I can't think about that.

Miss Paschonelle says it's normal, but I don't know. Mom started drinking seriously for the first time. It's serious when you prefer to drink alone. Everybody was always drinking in Florida, but she liked to collect her vodka and tonic and go out to the pool by herself so nobody would know how she was knocking them back.

Mr Bloomberg tried to reason with her, and then she'd start to cry. They would go in their bedroom and shut the door, but I would listen.

There's nothing for me to do, she says. My life is just a wasteland here. Everyone is so old. You're so old.

Arthur says I'm afraid nothing can be done about that. What about college? You said you wanted to go back to school.

What's the point? How can I make any friends there? They look at me and see an old married woman. I don't have any social options. Can't you see that? I'm just so completely tied down. The kids. You. You tie me down. I can't stand it.

I'd listen as long as I could bear it, and then I would knock on the door.

I said can I use your toilet? Mine's got a diaper in it. They had to shut up then.

Sometimes I wished she'd have a car accident. She could drive off a bridge and drown in the bay, and then there'd just be Mr Bloomberg and me and Stoppard. I thought everything would be perfect if that would happen.

That was a terrible thing to wish for. I knew it. I had to work myself up to that wish. I thought about wishing it, and then I'd back off because it was so terrible, but then finally I did wish it.

She got drunk on the patio. She threw up and then slipped in the mess and twisted her ankle.

Linda? Can you help me? I fell, she said.

I took the baby and went in the cement room. That was the little room by the kitchen where the hot-water heater and the air conditioner lived. Nobody ever went there.

I sat on the floor and held Stoppard on my lap.

Linda? she yells. Help me, Linda.

After a while she started to cry.

I wished she would just die.

In the sixth grade I joined the Barbies. That was a club. It was for girls. It was supposed to be for everyone, but the truth is you had to be cute. When you joined, they picked out a secret name for you. It was supposed to be a good one, off a fashion model or a character on television. When we were alone you were supposed to call people by their secret name. My name was Cindy, off the Brady Bunch.

I wanted to be Marcia. She is the oldest Brady girl.

But her name was already taken by Cindy Rodgers who was the founder and president of the club.

When I watched the programme I brooded about that. It seemed unfair. Marcia was what I wanted, and somehow I got stuck with Cindy's real name.

Cindy would say to me, Cindy you'd really look good in that pink top, or, it's Cindy's turn to pick out where we sit in the movie.

She called me Cindy every chance she got.

To think of the Barbies now makes me ashamed that I even wanted to be associated with such an outfit, but I'm being honest and reporting the bad with the good.

Miss Paschonelle says everyone has some stupid trick in their background.

The club lasted a year. Then the teachers found out about it and broke it up. It was causing too much misery. I was out of it by then for my own reasons, but while I was a member I didn't think about much else. It was as if there were two of me. The one in the club, and the other watching and admiring.

I thought I was having a good time.

Cindy and her mom used to pick me up with the other girls in a Buick Riviera and we'd go to the mall or to their house up at the lake and play tennis or water ski.

It was at the lake that we saw boys. They were the same boys as at school, but there they had no time for us. They had their sports and video games. They wouldn't even talk to you in the hall.

At the lake it was different. We played cards at night, and there was a game called flashlight. It was like hide and seek, only there were teams. You got tagged with a light. You were supposed to scream.

Sometimes a boy would ask you to go for a walk. They wanted to make out.

I wouldn't do that. The next morning at school you say hi and they act like they aren't sure who you are. Oh, hi, they say and then it's off to the videos.

There was a boy named Raphael that I liked. He was someone's cousin on a visit and only came to the lake one time. He lived in Boston with his dad.

He said he was going to teach me how to juggle.

He said you don't have to if you don't want to, but I can teach you how in thirty minutes.

He used scarves to begin with. The idea is that they float when you toss them up in the air, so you have time to catch them. The problem was we were on the beach and the wind was blowing the scarves away.

I fell over I was having such a good time. It was getting dark. I said lie down beside me and we'll look at the stars.

OK, he said. But don't get any ideas.

He was a very funny boy.

He told me about his family. That was sad. His father fell in love with a twenty-year-old. Raphael's mom couldn't handle it, so she moved to Santa Fe where she was studying to be a silversmith. The twenty-year-old moved in, and that was OK until she got sick. She had a terrible fungus that she'd picked up hitchhiking in Africa. It made her skin turn rotten and stink. It was just on her hands at first, but then it began to spread. The apartment reeked of her, and his father spent all his time hovering over her and talking to doctors. She didn't have any insurance and they were going broke on medical care. There was a sticky brown medicine that they were supposed to paint on her skin. It smelled awful, too. Raphael said it got up his nose. If he took a deep breath he could still smell it.

Once he woke up and thought he heard crying. The light was on in the bathroom, and when he looked inside he could see his dad sitting on the toilet. He was crying and jerking off at the same time.

I said that's the saddest story I ever heard. I meant it, too, but we just lay on our backs and laughed and laughed.

It's what you have to do sometimes.

Raphael said he couldn't stand it any more and was going to move out to Santa Fe with his mom. She had her problems but at least there was no smell.

When I got back to the house, the other girls asked me if I had a good time with Raphael. When I said yes, they all grinned at each other.

What's so funny?

He's a queer. Didn't you know that?

I was really disappointed, but I said so what? Maybe he likes me anyway. He's nicer than most of the jerks around here.

Cindy says if you're a pervert you can't be a Barbie.

She was really beginning to annoy me.

When Mom realized I had a rich friend, she sat up and took an interest.

As soon as I walked in the door she'd say who was that? She'd been hiding behind the curtain and seen the car.

Nobody. Just a friend.

She followed me into my bedroom.

What's the matter, she says. You never talk to me any more.

What do you want to talk about?

Well, can't you at least tell me about your friends? Why don't you ever bring them home? Are you ashamed of me? Is that it? Are you ashamed of your own mother?

I give her the look when she says that. She knows what I think. I don't have to say it.

She's sobered up the next time Mrs Rodgers stops by. She comes out to the car.

Mrs Rodgers? How do you do? I'm Sandra Bloomberg. I wanted to thank you for taking Linda to the lake on Saturday. She had a wonderful time.

She bends down so she can get a look at Cindy.

Hello, Cindy, she says. What a lovely haircut. Linda can't do a thing with her hair. It's like a wild beast.

She seemed to click with Mrs Rodgers. They saw each other socially a couple of times, and then Mom starts to work on getting us into the country club. She couldn't figure out why Mrs Rodgers wouldn't put us up for membership, but then Mr Bloomberg explained that he was the reason.

They don't allow Jews in the country club.

What? Mom says. But they have some black members. Carol and Stephen Hoyt are black.

Yes, the Hoyts are fine. But not the Bloombergs. They've got to draw the line somewhere, he says. He winks at me so I know he's joking. He says you let in one black couple, and that's it. Nobody expects any more of you than that. But you let in some Jews, and pretty soon the place is crawling with them.

Mom says you make me sick. Joking about a thing like that. Anyway, I'm not Jewish.

She goes into the house and gets a drink and comes back to the pool.

She says if there's one thing I hate it's racial prejudice. I just can't stand it.

Later that night she got very drunk. She came into my room and shook me awake. She had a gin and tonic in her hands, and I could feel the ice water splashing on my bed.

I don't want you hanging out with that Rodgers girl any more, she says. You understand? They're a bunch of bigots. You owe everything you have to Arthur. You know that, don't you?

I grab the drink before she can spill it all over me. She puts her head down on my stomach and starts to cry.

I don't know what to do, so I pat her head. That seems to help.

Oh god, she says.

The Barbies found out when my birthday was and started bugging me about the arrangements. I tried to be cool and think.

Well? Cindy says. Where's the party going to be? At the Port O'Call?

No.

Well where? At your house?

Yes . . .

Well? What are we going to do?

We can swim in the pool . . .

Oh god, that's boring . . .

Maybe she should get a band. Are you going to get a band?

Yes.

What kind of band? A rock band?

No . . .

What? What kind of band?

A jazz band . . .

I didn't tell Mom that I'd invited people to a party. I knew she would have one for me, but it wouldn't be the right kind.

Cindy wanted to know if there were going to be boys at the party.

No. No, my mom said no boys.

It's no fun without boys . . .

One of the other Barbies said I should get a stripper. A male stripper doing a dance . . .

There's going to be.

What?

A stripper.

How old?

Sixteen. His name's Shawn.

No there's not. You're just making that up . . .

Your mom wouldn't let you . . .

She's just making it up. There isn't going to be a stripper . . .

When the day came, we all got off the bus at my stop as arranged and walked up the street in our party clothes. I prayed to God.

Dear God, I said, please when I open the door, let there be a jazz band playing and Mom in a linen suit with pearls to welcome us. Arthur won't be there because he's Jewish. Please God, do this for me, and I will never ask for another thing.

I prayed so hard my heart felt emptied out. I thought it was going to work. I wanted the party so much I didn't see how it was possible He could let me down.

There wasn't anything, of course.

Mom was asleep in the deckchair by the pool. Her head was back and her mouth open. It was black inside. She'd been waxing her legs and passed out in the process. The insides of her legs were covered with wax up to the bikini line.

Cindy says is this some kind of joke?

Mom wakes up and stares.

Wha? she says. Wha?

She swings her legs off the deckchair and tries to grab some girl's hand, but they all back off.

Oh, girls, she says. A terrible thing has happened. Mr Bloomberg had a stroke. He fell down and couldn't move.

She looks at me and tears start coming down her face.

I was going to call the school and tell you, but somehow I couldn't.

She wipes her eyes.

I decided to wax my legs instead, she says.

Cindy called up her mother to come and get them. While we're waiting for her, Mom wanders around getting Cokes for everybody and telling them how sad it is, how sad it is . . .

She says of course we're praying for a complete recovery.

She'd forgotten about the wax on her legs. A piece had got loose and was flapping like some terrible wound.

All the girls were polite when they left. Cindy put her arms around me and gave me a hug.

She says we'll just have that old party some other day, OK? I just wish there was something I could do.

I knew she was just being sincere. I didn't care. I hated her by that time.

When they were gone, Mom says well I'm sorry your friends all had to arrive at such an awkward moment. I wish I'd known you planned to invite them over. We could have got some Dorritos or something.

How bad is he?

Arthur? Mom shakes her head. It's pretty serious. I really don't know.

Maybe he'll be OK, I say. Maybe he'll get back to normal.

That Cindy is such a sweet girl, Mom says. Hey, I know. Maybe I could take you and her to Disney World. I mean for your birthday. Would you like that?

I don't think so.

Why's that?

I don't like her.

What? How can you say that?

Because it's true. I hate her guts.

Hey. I don't want to hear that kind of talk. It's ridiculous. You can't hate somebody twelve years old. She's a nice kid. She's got a little . . . I don't know. Something. Charisma. I met her dad the other day. He invited me to play golf at the club. As his guest. What do you think of that?

I don't care.

I know. You don't care about anything. You're too busy hating people.

Mom sits down and picks at her wax.

Hate's a terrible thing, she says.

5

When Mr Bloomberg came back from the hospital, he had a thing about his eyes.

He says where's the mirror?

What mirror?

I want to see my face.

Your face is fine.

There's something wrong. There's something wrong with my eye. It feels like one of my eyes is gone.

That's nonsense, Arthur.

Where's the mirror?

Mom sent me to get a hand mirror, and he looked at himself.

Yes, he says finally.

He was cold and started wearing flannel shirts buttoned up to his chin. One of his hands curled up. It crept up his chest and played with his buttons. He couldn't read because of his missing eye, so I took over and would go through the *Wall Street Journal* in the morning. Only his eye wasn't really missing, of course. We sat by the pool, and he watched the jays in the birdfeeder.

I said shouldn't we be moving some funds into the bond market? I think we're headed for a recession.

Where's your mother?

She has a golf lesson.

Golf lesson? Why does she want a golf lesson?

She needs to get out, I told him.

I read him the figures. GM down three eighths. Zenith down a point and a quarter. Forty per cent of the office space in downtown Chicago is unoccupied.

I say hey. Do you want to go over to the Port O'Call? We could see Mr Shirmir and Dave Fine.

Arthur says no no. I put my trust in the wrong people.

You don't mean Mr Shirmir, do you? He called the other day and asked how you were doing. He says he knows about some good investments in the Pacific Rim. You want me to have him come over?

No, no. Where's your mother?

At the golf lesson.

Oh, yes . . .

He thought about that.

She needs to get out more, he says.

Yes. You want me to read the futures?

Why aren't you at school?

It's Saturday.

Mr Shirmir came to see him without being invited.

How are you doing, Arthur? We miss you over at the Port O'Call.

Yes, yes. Linda. Go get us some coffee.

When I got back with the coffee, Mr Shirmir was gone.

Arthur says go see if he closed the door.

The door was wide open. Heat was pouring in like hot syrup. A green lizard was on the doorstep. I stamped and it ran between my feet and got inside. I looked for it but couldn't find it. I had to give up because **Mr Bloomberg** began to call me.

Linda! Linda! Where are you?

When I got back to the pool, he was in a sweat.

Shirmir was looking at my eye, he said. He knows now. I told him to go away. I said I know what you're after.

What? What was he after?

No, no . . .

He's shaking. His bad hand creeps up and plucks at his buttons.

I said you want me to read you George Will?

Yes. Read George.

We hired a black woman to come in and help. Her name was Helen. She helped Arthur take his bath and get shaved. Mom stood in the bathroom door and watched. She was supposed to be learning how to care for Arthur herself and made little motions with her hands while she looked. As if she was the one giving Arthur a shave.

Helen says now look, Mrs Bloomberg. It's not so difficult when you get used to it.

Yes, yes, Helen. I can see that.

When he comes out of the bathroom, Mom runs away as if he is going to get her. She scurries over to the bedroom door and watches Helen get him dressed from there. She makes the little motions. Now she's zipping up a pair of pants and tying a tie. Now she's holding a coat so he can get his arm in it.

She was no use at all, really.

She moves into Stoppard's room. She unfolds the cot from the closet and sets it up in the middle of the floor.

She says I can't bear infirmity. It is simply something I cannot bear.

Well, somebody's got to take care of him, I told her.

You and Helen do it, she said. I'll take care of Stoppard.

That was the deal, but she didn't keep to her part. As soon as I got home from school, she was out the door.

Where you going, I say.

I have a doctor's appointment, she says.

I didn't believe that. I follow her out into the driveway.

You're sick all the time! I shout. You must be near death's door!

I liked Helen. When we got the work done, I'd put the kettle on and we'd make a cup of Nescafe. We'd sit at the kitchen table and let our shoulders go slump.

Lord, Lord.

I say is it hard to take care of old people?

No, it's not so bad. You just keep them clean and tidy like a baby. They're grateful, usually. You take care of your little brother, don't you?

Yes.

Well, it's a little like that. We're all God's creatures. I'll tell you something. Even the oldest person in the world is a newborn babe in God's eyes. That's what the soul looks like when you go to heaven. Mr Bloomberg's soul looks just like he did when he was a little tiny boy.

I said I thought maybe that's what I'd do when I grew up. Take care of old people.

Oh Lord, she says. I worry about you.

Why?

Why aren't you out playing with your friends? Don't you have any friends?

*

Suddenly there wasn't any money. I didn't know exactly what happened to it, but we couldn't find any except for a few thousand in a Dreyfus money market account. I also had my investments. I'd moved them into Vanguard Morgan Growth after Arthur had his stroke. That's a mutual fund with an interest in long-term growth. I didn't tell Mom.

She'd say where's that money Arthur gave you?

What money? I'd say and look stupid. I knew she'd never be able to figure out what I'd done unless I helped her.

She wrote a cheque on the money market account every month to put in the regular chequing account. The cheque had to be for no less than five hundred dollars. That was what we were living on.

I said but you're spending principal. You're not supposed to do that.

I was horrified, but she wouldn't listen.

One day she picks me up at school. She's got Stoppard in his baby seat in the back. She burns rubber pulling away from the curb.

What's wrong?

She turns and shows me her face. She's black and blue under one eye.

Arthur hit me.

What for?

I don't know! I was clearing the table. Just after lunch. I picked up his plate and carried it into the kitchen, and when I turned around he was standing right there. Right behind me. I said what do you want, and he hit me.

She was shaking.

Where are we going?

To see somebody.

We drive out to the country club, and she takes us in a golf cart right out to the third tee. I don't remember how she knew that was where Dr Rodgers was going to be, but she did.

When he sees her face he makes a face of his own as if somebody punched him in the stomach.

Glen, she says. We got a real crisis on our hands.

What? What happened?

Arthur hit me. He's gotten out of control.

Dr Rodgers shakes his head.

Maybe he should be institutionalized, Sandra. There comes a point where people with dementia simply can't be managed at home.

Mom looks at him like he was out of his mind.

What are you talking about? I can't go back there. You've got to do something right now.

Dr Rodgers told me to take Stoppard and go wash some golf balls. There was a little machine near the tee for that purpose. Inside was a sort of paddle with holes in it that went up and down between some scrub brushes. You stuck the balls in the holes and pushed them up and down in some soapy water. I held Stoppard up so he could work it. Then we dried off the balls on the towel that was hanging there from the hook.

When I could see that Mom and Dr Rodgers had finished their discussion, I gave him the clean balls.

Here you are, Dr Rodgers, I said.

Thank you, Linda, he said and walked away.

Mom drove us home. I don't know what Dr Rodgers did. I think he probably finished his golf game.

*

Mr Bloomberg was in the kitchen trying to open a can of salmon when we got back to the house. He didn't pay any attention when Mom tiptoed in and grabbed her purse off the counter.

Mom says to me go get packed. We're leaving in ten minutes.

Where are we going?

Hibbing. I don't have any choice.

No, I said.

No what?

No, I'm not going.

Well you can't stay here.

Yes I can. Somebody's got to take care of Mr Bloomberg.

You can't do that.

Helen and I can.

Helen's gone. I paid her off this morning. There isn't any more money. Don't you understand? There isn't any money! My god, you're like a half-wit sometimes.

I know you're supposed to stay here. If you handle him right, he's OK.

I can't stand it! Don't you understand? I can't stand it one more minute. You don't know how terrible it is being stuck with an old man. You don't know! You just don't know! Now listen, Linda. Here's the plan. We're going to walk out that door in five minutes. I'll stop down at the gas station and call 911 and tell them there's an emergency situation at this house. The police will come and they'll take better care of Arthur than we ever could. It's for his own good. Can't you see that?

You married him. You're supposed to take care of him.

She fusses with her purse.

We're not married really.

What? This was news to me.

That's just a fiction, I'm afraid. The point is that I really have no responsibilities here.

No, you don't, do you? You don't care about anybody. You just want to run around taking golf lessons.

That's not true. I've done the best I can.

You just run around with Dr Rodgers, I told her. I know what you do. It isn't just golf.

She slapped my face.

You don't talk to me that way, she says. I'm your mother.

I went and sat on the floor in the cement room. I could hear her calling me. Linda, she yells. You come here. Linda!

She was barging around knocking over the furniture.

I'm leaving, Linda! she yells. I'm going to go without you!

The door slammed. I thought she was faking it, but she wasn't. She really did leave.

I sat there for a long time, even after I knew she was gone. Helen must have tidied up before she left. All the cleaning supplies were neat on the shelf and the broom was hanging on its nail. I hung on to that comfort as long as I could, but finally I had to go out and face the consequences.

Mr Bloomberg was still struggling with the salmon can.

Is that you, Trudie? I can't get this can open.

I opened it up and made a salad with an avocado. I sat him down on the patio and explained how things were.

Mom's gone. She took Stoppard and went off to Hibbing. I'll stay here for a while and fix the food and stuff, but you have to behave. Is it a deal?

That's fine. You have to watch the door, though, Trudie.
You must have left it open. Just anybody can walk in.
Somebody tried to take some dishes. Some woman off
the street. I don't know. I told her to leave.

He stops talking and looks at me.

You're not Trudie, are you?

No. I'm Linda.

Oh, yes. Trudie's dead . . .

Oh Lord, I thought. But I had made my choice and
was stuck with it.

6

The next day he was nearly all right again. He wanted to know if he was behaving strangely, and I gave him the facts. I told him the money was all gone.

There's no money? he said.

No.

Where is it?

I don't know. You lost it or did something with it. I can't figure out what.

What about the car?

Mom took it. Listen, I said. I've got some money in my mutual fund and you still get your Social Security. We'll live on that for a while.

What fund is that?

It's the Morgan Growth. It's doing OK.

I showed him the papers, and he turned them around in his hands, trying to get them straight in front of his good eye.

I'll take care of things, I said.

Oh Christ, he said. He went through his pill bottles in his top dresser drawer and I asked him what he was looking for.

I had some pills. Some medicine.

He stops pawing at his medicine and frowns.

I have a daughter somewhere, but I can't remember her name.

Carol. She lives in St Paul. She's a lawyer.

Carol . . . You better call her.

Where's her number?

It's in the desk somewhere. You better call her.

I found the number in his address book and called her up that night. I introduced myself and she said yes? She says it very cool, as if I'm going to try and sell her something.

I said your dad's sick, and maybe you should come down and take care of things.

What's wrong with him?

It's hard to say. Sometimes he forgets things and acts strange.

She says is he there? Let me talk to him.

I put him on the phone, and he acts like there's nothing wrong. He says oh no, we're all fine. How are things up there?

He says we ought to talk more often.

When he hangs up he can't look me in the eye.

I said what's wrong with you? You make me look like an idiot.

Well, I'm sorry. There's nothing wrong really. I'm just a little upset. I can't bother Carol every time I get a little upset.

I saw there was no reasoning with him, so I let it go.

I moved some of the money from Morgan Growth into one of Arthur's old money-market accounts, and we'd draw on that for his chequing account at the bank. I used Bank by Mail. That's a convenience for people who can't get to the bank in person for one reason or another. I had an ATM card and we'd use that for ready cash. There was a machine at the convenience store just across the bridge.

I went through his room looking for money and found a bunch of letters stuffed down at the foot of his bed underneath the sheet. Some were from organizations like the American Red Cross and the Cancer Society thanking him for his magnificent gift. But most of the money went to two places. One was an organization called the St Paul Society. They sent a letter that said that a special reception was being held June 12th for those on the golden honour roll, and that a place at God's table had been reserved for him and one guest. In addition he was a life member at Life! Christian Resort and that a suite was guaranteed available for him whenever he wanted to drop in for a while.

There were some restrictions on this last offer, but I don't remember what they were.

Another was from a broker in New York called Turks Manning and Associates. It had a fancy letterhead, but the letter was written in ballpoint by somebody in a hurry. It said that Mr Bloomberg had been informed of the risks involved in such money transactions, and that any further correspondence should be directed to a law firm whose name I couldn't make out.

I asked him about the St Paul outfit.

It's for Jews. So your mother can join the country club. They've got pull. They can fix it. I talked to a young man on the telephone. He explained. I'm not Jewish any more.

What are you?

Christian.

Oh for god's sake, I said. How much did you give them?

I don't remember. It's in the book.

I never found the book, but I figured out eventually that he must have given away or lost over four hundred thousand dollars in the course of two months. I wrote all my findings down in a blue notebook. You can check it if you like. I think his daughter Carol probably has it.

I lived with Mr Bloomberg for about four months after Mom left. Here is how I spent the money from the Morgan account:

Mortgage and taxes: $3,886.00.

Electric: $412.00. This was high because there was a period when Mr Bloomberg insisted on leaving the patio doors open, even with the air conditioner on.

Food and Entertainment: approximately $700.00. I told him he couldn't watch television with all of those appeals for money because he got upset. So we rented a lot of videos.

There were some one-time bills whose amounts I don't remember exactly, but they could be checked. They're in the chequebook, and the companies have the records. There was the phone bill, which never was much, because I didn't make any long-distance phone calls after we talked to Carol.

There was a homeowner's insurance bill and also one for the car. I paid that, even though Mom had the car. If anything happened to her and Stoppard, I thought it was important that they be covered. There was also a water bill, but I don't remember how much it was.

I think that's about everything. I let the pool service

and cable lapse. We did our shopping at the Cracker Box. That was the convenience store that I mentioned. It cost more, but it was just across the bridge in St Pete so we could walk. Also it was open twenty-four hours a day and we did most of our shopping at about four in the morning. That was when Arthur would start to get restless. I would get him dressed and we would head out before anyone else was out of bed. One advantage of this arrangement was that we didn't attract a lot of attention. We had our own cart. It was from a discount store, but we weren't the ones who took it off the lot. We found it in a ditch.

We bought Lean Cuisine and bananas mostly. For lunch we'd sometimes have salmon or tuna salad. It was convenient. I like food convenient.

I kept him clean and tidy the way Helen did. A shower every other day. I'd sit him on his stool in the tub and hose him down. Then I'd put him in a terrycloth bathrobe and put him in the sun by the pool. When he was dry I would powder him up and dress him clean from the skin out. I tried to shave him at first but it wasn't worth the effort, and finally we just grew a beard. Laundry wasn't a problem because we still had the washer and dryer.

He got frantic and said I was keeping him a prisoner in his own house.

I tried to reason with him, but he slapped my face and ran around pushing the patio furniture into the pool. I went and sat in the cement room until I heard the front door slam. I peeked out and he wasn't anywhere. The pool was clogged with cushions, and his bathrobe was floating in the water too. I thought oh hell, he's drowned himself, but when I poked around with a stick I couldn't find him. Then I had a worse idea. He has run out of the house naked. I didn't want to chase a naked old man down the street, but I braced myself and went looking.

When I found him I was glad to see he'd had enough sense to put on his suit. He looked normal except his shirt wasn't tucked in underneath his jacket and he didn't have any socks.

He was in a hurry to get somewhere. I didn't try to stop him. I just followed at a safe distance. He walked round and round the neighborhood, but he couldn't find what he wanted. He'd get to a corner and stop and look. Then he'd tip in one direction or the other and take off like a wind-up toy. He walked very fast, hunching up his shoulder on one side and swinging his good arm.

Finally he gave up and sat down on a bench by the canal where rich people keep their boats. I sat down beside him as if it was a coincidence that I was there too. After a minute I said are you OK now?

He said do you know the way home?

Yes.

Oh god, he said and started to cry. A lady came up and asked what was wrong.

Nothing, I said. I can take care of it.

Arthur said yes, she takes care of me.

That lady wasn't convinced, but I wiped his face and led him away before she could make up her mind what to do.

He came just as good as gold.

When I got home I found out his left foot was all blistered because of no socks. I took care of that. I made him soak his foot in hot water until the blisters burst and then sit with it in the sun.

I fished as much patio furniture out of the pool as I

could. Most of it had sunk, and the pump was making a funny noise, so I shut it off.

The house was quiet then. Quieter than ever.

I stopped going to school. Arthur got nervous if I wasn't around. I was afraid a truant officer would come looking for me, but that problem took care of itself. The school called up and wanted to talk to Mom and find out what was happening. Mr Bloomberg answered it.

What? he said. Mrs Bloomberg? No, you can't speak to her. She's dead. Yes. Breast cancer. Yes, thank you. Thank you very much. No, my daughter lives in St Paul, Minnesota. No, I don't know her school.

When he hangs up he chews his lower lip.

That was the school, he says. They want to know why Carol isn't coming there any more. I told them I don't know.

That's OK I tell him.

She's got polio. That's why she's not in school. Should I call them back?

No, you don't have to.

I don't know the number.

It's OK.

I can't be responsible any more. What more does she want? She never forgave me for her getting polio. That's the problem.

No.

I looked at her legs in those braces. I couldn't bear it. They were just sticks.

It's OK.

I would do anything. She knows that. I can't turn back the clock. She should forgive me. It isn't fair.

*

80

After that the days blended together. It was like a dream. I'd get Arthur up at dawn and we'd cross the bridge to the store. Nobody was up in the neighborhood. The only people I talked to were some men who came to fish off the bridge. They were black. They showed me what they caught. Beautiful fish, all the colours of the rainbow. White people came later, but the fish they caught were grey and boring.

I don't have an explanation for this.

During the day I'd sit by the pool and read a book or watch nature take its course. With the pump off, the sun was sucking up the water from the pool. As the water level sank, some of the patio furniture Arthur had thrown in began to stick out. It was all covered with algae, and after a while I began to see little green frogs. I don't know how they got there. A bird must have brought one and it got away and multiplied. The lizard that got in when Mr Shirmir came to visit was there too. I dug up some of the paving stones from the patio and piled them up at one end of the pool so it would look more natural. I stuck some grass and ferns in the cracks, and sometimes I would run a hose over it like a little waterfall. It was really beautiful.

A girl came to the door and wanted to sell some Girl Scout cookies. I didn't know her, but suddenly I longed to see Myra Berkowitz again. I don't think I have mentioned her before. She was one of the Barbies too, but low man on the totem pole. Cindy said she got to join so it would look like anybody could get in if they wanted to badly enough.

After the Girl Scout was gone, I watched television and thought about how I might lure Myra over and keep her prisoner for a while. I thought I would write her a cheque and say this is for you if you stay overnight.

I couldn't decide what the right amount was. Fifty dollars didn't seem enough, and a hundred would scare her away. Finally I wrote her a cheque for seventy-five dollars. Pay to the order of Myra Berkowitz. I signed Mr Bloomberg's name because he was the one with the account.

I called her up on the telephone and said hey Myra. I'm having a party. You want to come over?

She says who is this?

It's me. Linda.

Oh. I thought you moved away.

No. I was away for a while. You want to come?

Can I bring somebody?

Who?

David Swartz.

No, this is just a girl party.

OK but I can't stay, she says. As if she had an inkling of what she was getting into.

I went to the Cracker Box and bought all the stuff Myra liked. Dorritos and bean dip and a Sara Lee banana cake. Two ripe mangos and a package of Dove bars for dessert.

I put Arthur in his bedroom with the TV, and then I turned on the hose in the little waterfall and set up a card table by the pool with some games on it. Chinese chequers and Monopoly.

I tried to think of everything. I planned that we would play some games and then just sit and talk for a while. I wanted to explain that I was sorry about the way she was treated in the Barbies. She would give me all the news and I'd say things that made her feel good about herself.

Of course this is not how things worked out.

When Myra showed up, I said well here you are.

I took her out to the pool and showed her the set-up. The bowl of Dorritos and the 7-Up cooling in an Igloo.

She says where is everybody?

Where's who?

Everybody else. I thought you said you were having a party.

I am. It's just you and me.

That's not a party. You can't have a party with just two people.

Yes, you can.

No, you can't.

I said oh shut up Myra.

I was beginning to remember how she irritated me sometimes.

I made her eat some Dorritos and we played a game of Chinese chequers. I let her win which was hard to do.

She leans over and says in a whisper what's your dad doing?

Who? Mr Bloomberg?

Yes. What's he doing?

I listen. I can hear Arthur singing along with the TV.

He's singing. He always sings along with this commercial. You want to play another game?

No. I think I better go home. I better call my mom to come get me.

No, I say, don't do that. I've got something else I want to show you.

I decided to be direct. I whipped out the cheque and showed it to her with her name on the line and the amount and the date.

I'll give you seventy-five dollars to stay overnight.

She starts to cry. She says what are you going to do to me?

I say what are you talking about? I'm not hurting you.

She screams don't hurt me!

It was almost comical.

I got her down on an air mattress and sat on her.

I'm not hurting you, I said. Read my lips.

She calmed down then. She said I could do what I wanted, as long as I didn't hurt her. I said OK, and when I got off she pushed her shorts down and pulled her shirt up over her face.

What are you doing? I said.

What? she says, peeking out at me. Isn't this what you want me to do?

No! I said, I don't want that. I'm not a pervert.

She said I'm not either.

Well pull your pants up, then.

I let her call her mom. We went out and sat on the front step and waited. It was getting dark out. The palmetto was rattling against the house. There was nobody on the street.

She was cheered up again. She says you know what? The teachers shut down the Barbies' club. They said it was causing too much heartache. I didn't care. You know something? Cindy Rodgers went all the way with Kevin Morissy and Brian Sonachuck the same day.

I tried to think of some interesting comment to make but couldn't come up with a thing. I really didn't care any more what Cindy did. I could hardly wait for Myra's mom to come and get her out of there.

After she left I went inside and found that Arthur was walking around the pool without his trousers. So it is just as well Myra went home when she did.

When I made him get dressed, he pushed me. He said that I'd turned the heat up and was trying to roast him alive.

Oh shut up, I said. I slapped his face. I had to jump up to do it.

I said oh shut up, you old fool.

That was the only time I was really mean to him, I swear.

When I got ready for bed I found that cheque for Myra in my pocket. I knew then that the whole idea had been nuts and I was getting as crazy as Mr Bloomberg. I tore up the cheque and resolved to be more sane.

Myra must have told about me being still around, because a boy came over. I'm not going to tell you his name. This was in Florida and it's all in the past. Nobody needs to know. Maybe when I'm in Florida next time I will look him up. Don't worry, I'll say. You were never implicated.

He said you want to do something?

What?

I don't know. We could take a walk or something.

I told him I couldn't. I had stuff to do.

I'll help you, he said.

No, I said. You could wait here, though. If you wait here I'll go with you.

He sat on the step outside while I went and fixed Arthur his supper. I set up a tray in front of the TV. I was so nervous my hands were shaking.

You stay here, I told him. I have to go out for a while.

That boy and I walked down to where the street ends at the water and sat on the stones there. It was getting dark. He said he loved me.

No, you don't.

Yes I do. I really do. I think about you all the time.

What do you think about me?

Nothing. I just really love you.

If you really loved me you'd take me to the movies, I said.

I will, he said. I really will.

No, I said. I can't go anyway.

After that we were boyfriend-girlfriend for a while. He would come over after Mr Bloomberg was asleep, and we'd pull an air mattress out by the pool and neck in the dark. Sometimes we kissed so much I got out of breath and then I would roll over on my back and watch the stars spin around.

What's the matter? he'd say.

Nothing. Nothing's the matter.

Come here, he'd say and pull me over.

I was really very fond of him.

I'm sorry to say that he was immature and couldn't keep a secret. He told some of his friends there wasn't anybody around but me and Mr Bloomberg.

They came over and rode their bikes back and forth outside.

Hey Linda, they called. Can we come in, Linda? I've got something to show you, Linda. What's this, Linda? You want to suck on it?

Mr Bloomberg sat up in bed. Trudie! he shouted. Trudie! I can't see! It's too dark!

I went and sat in the cement room until things calmed down.

In the morning a man came over and said he wanted to talk to my parents. He said he was Mr Vessy and lived next door.

They're not here right now, Mr Vessy. Can I help you, Mr Vessy?

He barges in past me.

Where's Mr Bloomberg, he says. I want to talk to him right now.

Arthur came out of his room blinking like an owl.

Yes, yes, he says.

Those young men, Mr Vessy says. Last night. It was terrible. We can't have that. It isn't that kind of neighbourhood. I won't put up with it.

No, Arthur says. No. Put a stick up it.

What? And look at your pool. I can't help noticing. That's a health hazard, Mr Bloomberg. You understand me? That has to be cleaned out.

Clean out your bum, Arthur says.

What?

Good, clean fun.

Yes, well, it has to be taken care of. No offence.

No, behind the fence. Put it up behind. All pumped out.

Yes. That's what I mean. All pumped out, Mr Vessy says and goes away.

I was afraid he'd call the city council, so I called the pool company and told them to come and fix things up.

The man they sent made a real fuss about the conditions things had gotten into and said we had to drain the whole thing. He fished out some of the furniture and turned on the pump.

He told me he hadn't had any breakfast and sure could use a cup of coffee. I got the hint and went to make him a cup of instant in the kitchen. I heard a yell, and when I came out I could see Mr Bloomberg in his bathrobe trying to fold up one of the chairs that had been pulled out of the pool. He was all covered with green algae. When he saw me he ran back in his room and slammed the door. I couldn't find the pool man anywhere.

Finally I looked in the pool. Most of the water had drained out by that time. I could see him lying on the bottom with his face in a green puddle.

I thought he was dead.

I ran and hid in the cement room and tried to decide what we should do. I could hear a scraping and a grinding noise and Mr Bloomberg grunting. I thought he must be disposing of the body, but when I peeked out I could see he'd pulled his old stationary bicycle out on the patio and was peddling away on it.

I went out and told him we had to call the police.

No, no, he says. I don't have time for that.

I could hear moaning. When I looked in the pool I saw the man was sitting up and holding his head. So he wasn't dead after all but merely stunned. His leg was broke, however, so I couldn't get him out of the pool by myself. I had to call 911, like it or not. While we were waiting, I made him a bologna sandwich. I hoped that if I was nice to him he'd keep his mouth shut, but it didn't work. When I lowered the sandwich down to him in the net on a pole, he just threw it against the wall and moaned some more.

When Emergency got him out of the pool he said Mr Bloomberg pushed him in. They wanted to know why he would do a thing like that, and the man said he was crazy.

Mr Bloomberg wouldn't get off his bicycle to be questioned. He just shook his head and pedalled faster and faster. So in the end they realized he was disturbed. They had an argument about whether to put him in the same ambulance as the pool man. The pool man shouted no no, keep him away from me.

I don't remember how it ended. I think they called him his own ambulance.

A policeman questioned me and then one of them asked if I had anyone I could stay with until they got in touch with Mom.

I said Myra Berkowitz and her family. It was a long shot but worth a try. The policeman let me put some clean underwear in a paper bag and drove me over in a cop car.

Mrs Berkowitz met us at the door and the officer explained the situation in a few words.

Mrs Berkowitz said well of course she can stay here.

She gave me a hug and everything.

She showed me Myra's bedroom and where the bathroom was. Myra's room had an extra twin bed in case a friend wanted to stay over, so I didn't feel like I was a burden.

I said where's Myra?

Myra isn't here. She went to a movie with her friend David. You want to have some supper?

No. What bed do I get to sleep in?

This one. Mr Berkowitz and I are watching the MacNeil-Lehrer Report. You want to join us?

No, I said and waited until she went away.

I could hear her talking about me to her husband. She says I don't know what to make of her. Is it all right to leave her in there by herself?

Mr Berkowitz says yes yes. Let her sort things out. She's all right. There's nothing we can do.

That seemed true to me.

I went in the bathroom and cleaned up and then I got in the bed and lay still.

Myra comes in later. She was all sweaty from her date with David Swartz and had to take a shower. When she was done, she snuck into bed with her bathrobe on and turned out the light.

I said well how was the movie?

She pretended she was asleep and couldn't hear me.

That was OK. I wanted to sleep myself, but I couldn't. Whenever I closed my eyes I would see the man being lifted out of the pool all white and bloody and Mr Bloomberg on his stationary bicycle pedalling away as fast as he could.

It was like a TV I couldn't turn off.

7

Miss Paschonelle says the judge is going to want to know why I busted out the window in my room at the Centre. I will now take a minute to explain.

First of all, it was an isolated incident.

Crystal Ramirez got back her **AIDS** results and she is HIV positive. She is the girl with the torn ear. It is OK for me to mention this because the news is no longer confidential. Her grandmother spilled the beans at home, and it got back to the Centre in about two minutes.

That's OK. Sister Mary Joseph explains you've got nothing to worry about unless there is an exchange of blood products.

Now how could that happen? she says. I want you girls to think.

Using each other's toothbrush.

Yes, that is one possibility, I suppose. But I want you to think of some others.

Nosebleeds. You could have a cut on your hand and she bleeds out of her nose into it . . .

Yes. You come tell me if Crystal gets a nosebleed. What else? When do you puncture the skin?

Tattoos . . .

When you pierce somebody's ears . . .

*

That was me. I thought of that.

Yes, exactly. This means no body piercing and no tattoos, Crystal. You understand? Nobody's supposed to pierce her, and she's not to do any piercing. Because what if she was piercing your ear or something and pricked her finger? That could be serious.

Jackie Cochran says is it all right to touch her, and Sister Mary Joseph says well, of course, but Jackie keeps flapping her lip. Because, she says, Crystal let Linda touch her.

No, she didn't, I say. But nobody believed me. Sister Mary Joseph told Jackie that was enough, but the seed of suspicion was planted, and Sister Mary Joseph took me aside later and asked for an explanation.

There was really nothing to it. It was just that for a long time I wanted to touch Crystal's torn ear. I sat in the cafeteria and looked at it, and my throat closed up so I couldn't eat. I tried to put it out of my thoughts, but that was no good so finally I asked her. I said can I touch your ear. It was early in the morning before wake-up.

All right, she said and let me get in bed with her. I touched her ear. It was soft except for the torn part which had a tough edge.

I asked her if it hurt, and she said no, it was all healed up now. Her mom wanted to get it fixed, but to do that would take an operation. Crystal wasn't sure she wanted to bother.

I said no, it looks good.

You think so? she says.

Yes, I said. Anyway thanks for letting me touch it.

She said I could touch it some more if I got desperate.

She is a true friend. When I leave here I hope we can visit sometimes.

A girl cousin is the one that tore her ear. Crystal had on an earring, and that girl stuck her finger in that and tore it out. She did that because her boyfriend kept talking about how Crystal was going to be a real babe in a couple of years.

It bled down her dress, front and back. Her dad wouldn't take her to a doctor because he was an illegal immigrant. He tried to patch it up with adhesive tape, but that didn't work, so it healed torn.

So you can see there was no exchange of blood products when I touched her. Nothing like that. You can check up on her dad if you want to check up on somebody. He probably had blood all over.

Sister Mary Joseph said that's fine. She said I was clearly a good friend, and I should keep an eye on Crystal and help keep her out of trouble. She says Crystal is so good-natured that sometimes people talk her into things that are bad for her. I said I would. So that is one of my responsibilities now.

Sister Mary Joseph knows that I'm not very good-natured, so I'm the man for the job.

But we had this conversation after I busted out the window.

When I found out that Crystal had HIV, I felt really bad about it. I sat on my bed and watched her fluff up her pillow with her greeny yellow hands and thought about what I should do. She had told me who the guy is who gave it to her, and I decided I would kill him with a gun. Someone ought to do it, and it seemed to me that I was the obvious choice. I had no motive and I'd wait until Crystal had a good alibi. My first plan was that I would say hello James (not his real name). Did you know that you gave Crystal the AIDS virus?

I thought I would give him a chance to be sorry and beg for mercy, and then I'd say very calmly, sorry, that's not good enough. You got to go. And then Bang Bang, I'd shoot him in the heart.

I thought about this for a while, but then I got worried because what if while we were talking he got rescued or saw his chance and grabbed the gun away?

Also, what if he said go ahead? You would be doing me a favour. I have great remorse about hurting Crystal and I would kill myself but I'm too much of a coward.

What if he said that? Then I would be weakened and not able to do it. I don't think I could kill someone who had real remorse.

So I decided I would just shoot him without any warning and the world would be better off.

I felt good after I made that decision, but then I realized. What if I did shoot this boy? That would be like thinking I know what's best for everybody. I would be acting just like Frank Perry.

This was an important insight, according to Miss Paschonelle, but at the time I felt thwarted. That was why I broke the window in our room and the lights in the hall.

It was premeditated, so I can't plead insanity. I waited until Crystal left so she wouldn't get any of the blame. She said are you coming to breakfast, and I said in a minute. She said I'll wait a minute, but I told her to go ahead. I need to be alone. So she said OK and went. That is one good thing about this place. When you want to be alone nobody says hey what's the matter with you?

Everybody's got something wrong in here and has to get off by themselves occasionally.

When I knew Crystal had probably got to the cafeteria with twenty eyewitnesses to testify, I busted out the windows with a chair. The cold air came in, and some people going by outside stopped in their tracks to look at me. They all looked like dopes with their mouths hanging open. Hey you dopes, I said, what are you staring at? I threw a pillow out the window and a man grabbed it and ran away. I'm not kidding. He must have been homeless and really in need to steal one of those flabby pillows. I threw some other stuff out, and Sister Angelica came in and tried to sit on me, so I went out to the hall and smashed a couple of lights before I was controlled.

So that is why I broke the window in my room. I am now sorry for doing this stuff. I really mean it. I was even sorry at the time I was doing it, but, as Miss Paschonelle explains, I did not have a good vehicle for expressing frustration.

Now when I'm frustrated I either vacuum or write in this report. I prefer vacuuming and sucking up the dirt that gets spread all over the television room. I like to find a real gritty patch. The vacuum makes long, clean rows and you can see results right away.

Sister Mary Joseph says as long as there is dirt, the windows are safe. She is a good person, really, and knows how to lighten the mood.

When Mom showed up in Florida, she looked good. She'd gained some weight and had her hair cut. It came down in flat licks around her face. She had on a new suit. She told me it was made out of sharkskin, but I checked it out later and it was just ordinary fabric.

She picked me up at the Berkowitzes' and we went back to Arthur's house in a cab. On the way she looks out the window.

Look at those palm trees, she says. They look like giant dish mops. I'd forgotten how ugly everything is down here.

I asked her how everybody was in Hibbing, and she told me she didn't live there any more. I met someone, she says. I think I might get married again.

I didn't want to hear that.

Who is it? I said. Is it Dr Rodgers?

No! What made you think of him? I almost forgot all about him.

Because if it's Dr Rodgers I'm not going.

I said it wasn't, didn't I? His name is Frank. Frank Perry. You don't even know him.

Well, who is he? Where'd you meet him?

Oh, I've known him for years. He's an old friend.

She can't look me in the eye when she says that. She knocks on the driver's security glass.

Could you turn up the air-conditioning, please? she says. We are suffocating back here.

When we got to the house the first thing she did was look in the pool. The mess in the bottom had started to dry out. It had cracked and turned colours. It wasn't bright green any more. It was mould colour. I don't know what happened to the frogs. They must have died. The bologna sandwich was still there. It looked fresh. The mustard was bright yellow.

Is that where he was? she says.

Who?

The man. The man who fell in the pool.

Yes. Are we going to stay here?

Just for a couple of days. I don't know. We'll have to see. I have to go see a lawyer tomorrow. Carol Bloomberg's having a fit about that money. You sure that Arthur gave it all away?

Yes. I got the letters.

Good. Don't turn on any of the lights. I don't want the neighbours to know I'm here. We'll just go to sleep in your bed when it gets dark.

She takes off her top. When she turns around I can see she's started another baby.

I don't say a word.

Well just what is that look supposed to mean? she says.

Whose baby is that? I say.

Don't talk to me in that tone, she says. I told you I met someone. It's not the end of the world. He's dying to marry me. All I have to do is say yes. Anyway, what are you so sour about? It's my child. Frank's happy about it. It would be nice if you could at least put on an act. Did Arthur see you like that?

Like what?

Like that. Half naked.

I don't know. Sometimes.

Mom peeked out the window through the venetian blinds. It was getting dark outside.

We can turn on the lights, I told her. It'll be OK. Nobody will notice. They're all inside watching TV this time of day.

She lets go of the shade and turns around to look at me. Did anything happen while I was gone?

What sort of thing?

You might as well tell me. I'm going to have a doctor

examine you when we get home. He'll be able to tell if a man's done something to you.

Nobody did anything.

I don't think I could stand it if I thought that crazy old man had been doing things to you.

I already said he didn't.

She got into bed and pulled the sheet up under her chin. We'll find out, won't we? When we ask the doctor.

They can't tell. Not really.

Of course they can. They look at you down there, and they can tell exactly what you've been doing.

No, they can't.

You believe what you like. I'm just telling you the facts.

8

That was my first time on an aeroplane. I don't think it showed. I stayed cool. The airline stewardess stood up and told us how to fasten our seatbelts and what to do if some little yellow cups fell out of the ceiling.

You put one over your face and breathe normally. Don't worry if the plastic bag doesn't inflate. It's not supposed to.

Just before we land Mom squirts perfume down her front and makes me comb my hair.

Now listen, she says. You're going to have to behave yourself. Frank didn't know about you until just a few days ago. I meant to tell him, but I kept putting it off. Finally it was too late. It reached a point where if I told him the truth, it would look like I'd been keeping you a secret.

She touches her stomach with her fingers. It isn't easy, she says. Two kids and now this.

Are you sure he knows about me now?

Well of course he does. I said so, didn't I? What's the matter with you? You're so suspicious.

She feels her stomach again. I won't kid you, she says. I wish this hadn't happened.

Frank and Stoppard were waiting at the gate. Frank had

his hair cut short on top and long in the back. He had a little diamond in one ear. So that was his fashion statement. Someone who is supposed to be grown-up dressing like a punk. I wouldn't even look.

I told Sister Mary Joseph they ought to have those machines at the airport set to catch crazy people. When Frank walks through, the alarm sounds and Security rushes up with guns drawn. He makes a break for it because that is the way he is.

Down he goes in a hail of bullets.

I wouldn't care. That's what I told her. I wouldn't care one little bit.

She says I don't want to hear that kind of talk, Linda. You should work on forgiving Frank. Not hating him.

Crystal had a splinter in her foot from running down the hall barefoot and Sister was trying to dig it out before it got infected.

Let God forgive him, I said. That's His business.

Sister Mary Joseph put the needle down and gave me her full attention. She says that won't do. I know he did a terrible thing, but you have to learn how to forgive. I know it is hard work. But if you could imagine the despair in his soul in those last minutes, then all this hate and anger would melt away. Hate makes us small, Linda. A soul that feeds on hate shrinks up into a hard little ball of hopelessness.

She takes my shoulders and gives me a shake. Do you believe me, Linda?

Yes, I say. I believe.

We didn't talk about it any more. I held Crystal down and she dug the splinter out. But I felt better so I know she is right. Now I work on forgiving Frank when I can stand to think about it. After lunch on Sunday is a good time. I lie on my bed and look at the ceiling and think about the past.

Frank lived in a little neighbourhood on the edge of town. It is just the one street. It turns off the highway at the Mobil station and then drops down toward the river. Across the river is the parking ramp for the university hospital. I could see it from my window.

He worked for a company that installed replacement windows. He didn't have a lot of money but owned his own house. He called it a handyman special. That makes it sound as if it was something you'd have to pay extra for, but all it means really is that it was in bad shape and needed a lot of work. The front porch was falling off and the walls were cracked, but he was going to fix it up and sell it for a profit.

That was one of his plans for getting rich. The other was that he was going to start his own business selling lawn ornaments cut out of plywood and painted to look like farm animals. He told me all about it that first night after Mom and Stoppard went to bed. We were sitting in the kitchen and drinking coffee and eating Sara Lee carrot cake out of the pan with our fingers.

Look at this, he says.

It was an article in a craft magazine. There was a picture on the cover of a ranch house with about fifteen cut-out cows and sheep on the lawn.

Read the highlighted part, he says.

J. P. Dimwiddy of Carlyle, Pennsylvania grossed four thousand three hundred dollars in his first month using the PressEase patterns for creating adorable livestock.

101

He is currently expanding production to meet an anticipated 20 per cent increase in orders.

He told me he'd sent for the plans and was going to start making cut-out farm animals himself in a couple of weeks.

Of course I don't expect to make as much as the man in Pennsylvania, he says. Not the first month.

I said where did you meet Mom, anyway?

He laughed. On the Interstate in Georgia. That old Caddy of hers threw a rod. I gave her a lift, and you know the rest.

What were you doing in Georgia?

Florida. I was coming back from Florida. I went down there after those storms on the east coast. I was doing some freelance construction.

You like it down there?

Hate it. Even the grass there has claws. Didn't talk to a soul for two weeks. I like it here better. You'll like it too. Don't believe what people tell you about the weather.

We finished up the carrot cake and he got some Hostess Twinkies out of the cupboard.

You know I didn't even know about you until a few days ago, he says.

Yeah. Mom said. You mind?

No! You're like a . . . What's that special surprise you get at Christmas? A bonus. You're like a bonus.

He sat back and smiled.

I will be honest. That first night I thought things might work out.

I was glad to see Stoppard again. I strip-searched him

the first chance I got. He was clean enough on the outside but filthy underneath.

I said my god, don't you ever change your underwear?

This is all I got, he said.

I gave him a bath and put him in some of mine. He didn't want to wear girls' but I said no arguments. Who's going to know?

In the morning I got up early and walked to the Krogers. I bought him brand-new underpants. Fruit of the Loom. With my own money. A package of three pairs for four sixty-nine.

They had a sale on doughnuts, so I bought a dozen of those too.

When I got home I put them on a plate. I told Frank this is my contribution to breakfast.

He said you don't have to contribute anything.

No, I said. I don't want you to think I'm a freeloader. I'll pay my own way while we're here, if that's all right with you.

No, I don't mind, he says. You could tell he was impressed.

Of course I didn't really pay my own way, but I'd bring home stuff every now and then. He liked potato chips. We tried out all the flavours. Sour cream and chives. Barbecue.

I brought home a bag of mesquite flavoured. I said I thought you might like to try these. I don't know if they're any good. It's just an experiment.

They're great, he says. Really good.

You don't have to eat them if you don't like them.

No, really. They're really great.

No, I can tell you don't like them. I'll throw them out.

Like hell you will, he says and gets his fingers in my ribs.

He won't stop until I give up and let him keep the chips.

It got on Mom's nerves that Frank and I got along so well. She says will you stop sucking up to Frank? You're turning into a little creep. Did you know that?

She had to lie down in the afternoon because Tyler gave her high blood pressure. We kept the windows open so she could breathe. The wind made the curtains snap.

I said don't you tell me what to do. I said I know whose baby that is. That man never loved you. He just saw his opportunity and took it.

She started to cry then, but I hardened my heart and walked away.

She couldn't lord it over me. Not with her record.

I went back to school. I caught the bus up by the Mobil. It was still dark out when it came. The lights flashed red and yellow and all the traffic had to stop. Inside smelled like bag lunch and boys. I made a friend right away. I wasn't antisocial. You can check. I sat in the back with Eileen. She kept a sharp pencil in her hand. If a boy tries to slam you in your seat, you hold the pencil so he stabs himself.

One day we took off our bras. We did it under our jackets so no one could see. We waved them around and a boy stole mine and threw it up in front. Mrs Seaforth came back from the front of the bus. The bra was in her hand. Someone had tied it into a knot.

All right, she says. Now whose is this?

No one says a word.

Jennifer? she says. I've got my eye on you.

We all look accusingly at Jennifer. Her dad brought her to the bus stop every day. He gave her a big squeeze before she got on.

It's not mine, Mrs Seaforth!

Whose is it then?

Linda's!

Oh! I say. That is such a lie, Mrs Seaforth. I still got mine on. I can show you, Mrs Seaforth.

That won't be necessary, Linda. Jennifer? You come up and sit in front with me.

Oh, Jennifer says. I don't even wear a bra, Mrs Seaforth. I just got an undershirt.

It was so great. We nearly died laughing.

At home I had to rub Mom's back. The baby was too big and she had a lot of discomfort. She lay on her side and I dug my knuckles in.

This is the last one, she says. Never again.

Her hands and feet swelled up. She got her rings off just in time. We had to use soap. The doctor said a few more days and the rings would have cut off the circulation. Her fingers would have turned black and fallen off.

Her water bag broke, but labour didn't start. She was frightened then. She thought she'd die with that giant baby stuck in her. I woke Frank up and he took her to Emergency. That was the plan anyway because there was no insurance. In the morning he came back. He said everything was OK. It was a baby boy.

Mom brought the baby home and laid him on her bed. He was wrapped up in a paper blanket. She opened him up so Stoppard and I could see. He was bright red with a big head and stomach and scrawny little legs and arms jerking back and forth. He looked like a wind-up.

The microwave buzzed and she went to check it.

Change Tyler, won't you? she says.

That was his name. Tyler.

I went and sat on my own bed. I wasn't going to take care of that baby. I could hear him squealing and Stoppard making hushing noises.

You stay away from him, Stoppard! I shouted, but he ignored me.

When Mom came back she got really mad.

What are you doing? she says. Didn't I tell you to take care of the baby?

You do it, I said. Call up Cindy Rodgers and ask her. It's her brother. Not mine.

Mom closes the door so Frank and Stoppard can't hear.

She says you keep your mouth shut about those people. You understand? I'm not going to tell you again. This is no joking matter.

All right, I say, but I'm not taking care of that baby.

Who asked you? she says. You think I need your help? I don't need you at all.

That attitude didn't last long. One Friday I came home from school and she was waiting for me. She was all dressed up in her sharkskin suit and pantyhose. She said she had to go downtown and see some people. She'd already made supper. It was on the stove.

Who? I said. Who are you going to see?

None of your business. How much money have you got?

I don't have any.

Don't lie to me, you little nit. Do you think I'm an

idiot? I know you cleaned out Arthur's bank account before we left.

She made me show her one of my hiding places. I will tell you since it is no secret now. It was in the window frame in my room. It's that space where the weights run up and down. You get to it through a little door held down with a screw. You undo the screw with a dime and reach inside.

I took out the ziplock bag with the money and gave it to her. She reached in the hole herself and felt around to make sure she'd got it all. She wanted to know if I had any other hiding places, but I told her no.

You little liar, she says, but let the matter drop. There was enough in the ziplock to keep her happy for a while. Sixty-two dollars and some change. She took the paper and left the rest for me.

She went out and sat on the porch step with the baby until Frank got home. When he pulled into the drive she went out to meet him. I could see them talking. After a minute she gave him the baby and he gave her the keys and she got in the truck and drove away.

Frank came into the house.

Your mother has an appointment. A job interview. She said we should eat without her. What is that smell?

Curry.

He juggled the baby with one hand and stirred the pot on the stove with the other.

Well, this looks really delicious, he says.

I woke up in the middle of the night. I could hear the baby screaming. I went downstairs. Frank was in the kitchen trying to give him a bottle, but he didn't know how. He made the bottle too hot. It would burn the baby's throat.

Give me that, I said. I grabbed Tyler and held the bottle under the cold water.

Your mom's not back, Frank says. It's after one. Do you think something happened?

No, I said.

Maybe we should call the police.

No!

I don't understand, he says. I thought things were going so well.

She gets upset sometimes.

Well, if she thinks she can just waltz out of here anytime she gets upset she's got another think coming, he says.

I thought he was really going to get tough, but it was all just talk.

She came back when we were having breakfast. She was sober, but looked worn out and dusty, as if she'd been walking all night. I never did find out what happened to my sixty-two dollars.

She poured a cup of coffee and stared out the window over the brim. Nobody dared say a word. Stoppard tried to cuddle up, and she slapped his head.

Get away! she says. My skin hurts.

Frank finally worked up enough nerve to ask her where she'd been, and she jumped down his throat.

I don't have to tell you! I don't have to tell you anything! she says. It's none of your business.

But we were worried sick . . .

Well, that's your problem, isn't it? I was having a crisis, Frank. A crisis. Don't you understand?

She threw her cup in the sink and stomped upstairs. Frank hung back for a while and then he went up too. I could hear them going from room to room, slamming doors, shouting and crying. I tried to get Stoppard to go outside, but he wouldn't leave. He sat in his chair and hung on to the bottom with both hands. After about ten minutes things calmed down.

When they came downstairs they were holding hands and he had a big smile on his face.

He said they had set the date. They were going to get married in October.

We wanted you guys to be the first to know, he says.

Great, I said.

Miss Paschonelle asked how I felt about that.

What do you mean?

Were you happy? Sad? Afraid? What?

I didn't feel anything, I told her. I knew it wasn't going to happen.

That same day Frank brought Tyler in his bassinet into my room. He set him down in the corner by the window.

I thought I'd bring the baby in here for a while, he says. Your mom needs to sleep. Is that OK?

Yeah.

Just for a couple of hours.

I said all right.

He tiptoes back down the hall and shuts their door behind him without a sound.

They never did come back and get that bassinet. Tyler has been in my room ever since. I'm not going to complain about that, though. It really is for the best.

9

I told Sister Angelica it was a miracle that Jack and I ever met.

She didn't like that.

A miracle reveals the hand of God.

But what I meant was if you list up all the things that had to happen first, it's practically everything. It's practically my whole life.

I told Jack that. I said what if Arthur Bloomberg hadn't lost his mind that time and Mom hadn't come back north and got hooked up with Frank? I wouldn't be here.

He says yes. Looked at in a certain way, the whole history of the world seemed arranged so we could meet that first time.

He said we were doomed by circumstance. Our fate was in the facts.

Sister Angelica says that is just an excuse. We have Free Will. We must choose the good and not the bad. You should never have talked to that man, Linda. You should have turned your face away when he approached you.

*

Sometimes when I was with Jack I'd pretend I couldn't remember when that was. When I should have turned my face away.

You were in your front yard, he says. Turning cartwheels in the sprinkler. Don't you remember? You and Stoppard.

So it must have been summer.

Of course it was summer! Don't you remember? I stopped the car and I said are those cows for sale? You remember. Those farm animals Frank made out of plywood. I asked you if they were for sale.

That was just an excuse to talk to me. Right?

Right.

You would have done anything. Asked directions or something like that if there weren't any cows.

Right. I would have grabbed you and stuffed you in the trunk if I'd had the nerve.

Well, I don't remember any of this. What did I say?

You said yes. Yes the cows are for sale. You were standing there in your swimsuit. Your legs were wet. They were covered with grass clippings. You had a mosquito bite on your ankle. While we talked you scratched it, and it started to bleed. Are you sure you don't remember?

No. I don't remember.

You stood there telling me about cut-out cows and all I wanted to do was bite you in the ankle. First your ankle, then your neck.

What are you? A vampire?

Yes. I want to suck your blood. All your bodily fluids.

You are so gross, I tell him. Were you alone?

Yes.

Wasn't Elizabeth with you? I seem to remember that Elizabeth was with you.

No. I was alone.

He didn't like to talk about Elizabeth. Whenever she came up in the conversation, his face would smooth out as if someone had ironed it flat.

I remember now, I say. She wanted a cut-out cow. She wanted two cows for her birthday.

No. I bought them for her as a surprise. She wasn't there.

But you invited me to come to her birthday party.

Yes.

Not just me. Everybody. Mom. Frank. Stoppard and the baby. It would have looked weird if you'd just invited me. You remember.

Yes.

So that's how I got to Elizabeth's birthday. There were a bunch of kids I didn't even know. She said to everybody, come on. I want to show you something.

She led us down the hill towards a dark grove of trees. She was wearing a white dress. It was getting dark. The grass under our feet was wet and the air was filled with lightning bugs.

The other kids got distracted and ran off. I could hear them shouting. I kept my eye on Elizabeth in her white dress. I wanted to see what she would do.

After a while there was just her and me.

She had a little flashlight. It was the kind that a person has on a key chain so she can find the door lock on the car.

She said stand still.

She walked away from me a little bit and then began

to flash the light on and off. She did it in time to the lightning bugs. They swarmed around her. She didn't move. They crawled in her hair and over her hands. Hundreds of them.

They are in love with me, she says. I'm the queen of bugs.

That flashlight was a birthday present. It was what she asked for. She needed it so that she could talk to the bugs. She got other stuff, of course. Her own video camera and a graphite tennis racket. We gave her a cut-out chicken, thrown in for nothing with the cows. She sent us a note later. Thank you for the lovely chicken. I will always treasure it.

I didn't really believe that, but it's the thought that counts.

Her mom never came out of the kitchen during the whole party. I don't want to say anything bad about her but she is a strange person who cooks all the time. She had on an old apron and her hair was coming down in sweaty loops. I thought she was the caterer.

What are you doing in here? she says.

Nothing.

Out! she says and gives me a swat.

I hung around with Jack after that. He must have found out from Mom that I had an interest in finance.

What do you like in the market? he says.

I don't know. I haven't kept up. Technologies looked good a couple of months ago.

They still look good, he says, but I'm nervous. This market just keeps going up. It seems crazy to me. I'm worried about a correction. A really heavy correction, if you understand.

Listen, I said. Inflation's low. The economy is still expanding. The market's OK. You haven't lost a penny until you sell.

He nods. Hey. I think you might be right, he says and we grin at each other.

On the way home, Frank drove too fast. The headlights saw grass and trees, not the road. He had to put on the brakes.

Mom says what is the matter with you now?

Nothing. You and that Green guy got along pretty well.

Don't bore me, Frank. We talked about real estate. That's his business. I also am interested in real estate.

She looked out the window at the dark.

He said he thought they might find something for me to do at Persic Realty, she says. He could help me get a licence. He thought I'd be good at it.

You think that's a good idea? Who's going to take care of the baby?

Mom swivels round to give him a hard look.

You really are an idiot, Frank. This is a real chance for me, she says calmly. If you screw it up I'll kill you.

She wouldn't talk to us after that. When we got to the house she shoved Tyler at me and went upstairs and locked herself in the bedroom. Frank stood at the bottom of the stairs and yelled at her.

That guy's not so smart. He says how much are the cows? Two hundred, I told him. Each? he says. I told him there was a seventy-dollar installation fee if I did the work. Each? he says.

Frank licks his lips.

114

Mr Each? That's what I should call him if he's so smart.

We listen, but she doesn't say a word.

For god's sake, Frank says. He heads for the garage. After a while I heard the band saw start up and I knew he was ripping out more cows.

10

Miss Paschonelle and I use that little room near Sister Mary Joseph's office to talk private. I get there first because she is usually late. I can hear her coming down the hall, her heels clicking. Slow down, Franny, Sister says. It can wait. They both laugh.

She comes in and takes off her coat and scarf. When she shakes out her hair I can tell the weather outside even if I don't already know. Today she brings in a smell of snow.

We go over it all again. About how Jack and I started seeing each other. I've really tried to tell her everything. But somehow it's never enough. It's as if there's something important that I've left out, but we don't know what it is.

But why, Linda? she says. Why?

I don't know. We really hit it off. I liked him a lot. Can't I say that?

What?

About liking Jack.

Is it true? she says. I want you to think carefully.

Oh yes, it's true. He was really personable.

She has to have a cigarette. You can't smoke in the Centre. She has to go outside and stand by the front

116

door. If I lean out the window I can see her shivering and puffing away.

You're going to kill yourself with those things, I tell her.

Elizabeth called up and said I think you're supposed to come over.

OK I said.

She had her own room on the third floor with a fireplace. There was only one skinny bed. If someone slept over, they would have to sleep on the floor or on the couch next to the window.

She had a friend there already. Her name was Justine. They were using the couch to practise how to sit down.

Like this, Elizabeth says. She lets her butt down like there is a sore place on it and folds her hands.

Justine does the same thing, only she leans back and puts her arm out along the back of the couch.

That looks nice, says Elizabeth. The arm stretched out like that.

Thank you.

No, I'm serious. You have very attractive arms, Justine. I have too much flab.

Justine says no, you don't. What I worry about is this. She touches her armpit. Some people are very unattractive here, she says. Even people who are nice otherwise.

Oh, I know, says Elizabeth. She thinks a minute. Kathy Phelps, she says.

Yes, exactly. She should never wear anything sleeveless.

No. When she puts her arm down the skin folds up. It reminds me of something. It looks . . . I don't know . . . weak.

Where's your dad? I said.

They look at each other and laugh.

What's so funny?

Nothing, Elizabeth says. Did you want to talk to him about finance?

I went downstairs but I couldn't find him. I talked to Mrs Green in the kitchen. She blinked at me and wiped her fingers on her apron.

Well, Linda. Here you are. Are you having a good time with Elizabeth and Justine?

Yes.

I asked her what she was doing. The counters were covered with cheesecakes. She told me she was writing a cookbook and had to try out all the recipes.

She says this one is made with jalapeños. I know that sounds crazy, but it's interesting. You want to try it and tell me what you think?

I ate some but didn't like it. It was hot. I said excuse me, and went in the little bathroom by the front door and spit it out. I would have swallowed it if I could, but I couldn't. The truth is I didn't like any of her cheesecakes. Some I said were delicious, but she knew I was lying. I couldn't make my mouth work right when I tried to eat them.

She went down the hall to a room where Mr Green was. He'd been there all the time and I didn't even know it. She told him to take me home.

She said I'm really very busy right now, Jack. I can't deal with these distractions.

Oh, I'm sorry, darling. I didn't realize . . .

You just don't seem to understand how much concentration this work requires.

Oh, no. Of course. If you're busy . . .

For heaven's sake, that's what I'm telling you, Jack.

In the car, Mr Green says put your seatbelt on.

No, I said. I hate those things. I slapped his hands when he tried to buckle me in.

It's for your own good.

I don't care. Where were you? I said.

What do you mean? I was right there.

No, you weren't, I said. You were supposed to be there. They were laughing at me.

Who?

Elizabeth and her friend. They were laughing at me.

No, they weren't. I'm sure they weren't.

How would you know? You weren't there.

He rolls his eyes. I think I'd better take you home now, he says.

No! I don't want to go there.

I think you'd better.

No! I said. I reached over and gave the wheel a jerk so he couldn't turn when he wanted.

We nearly ran into a tree. He slams on the brakes and I slide under the dashboard. He drags me up by the arm and gives me a shake. There, he says. That's what I mean. Now put on your seatbelt.

He buckles me in and gets his hands all over me in the process.

I felt calm then. You are such a coward, I said. You really are.

He didn't take me home. We drove down a bumpy road. There were tall trees and a brick wall. I don't know where it was. We stopped at a big house with chimneys. We got out of the car and looked at the windows. They were made of little diamond pieces of glass.

Tudor. Five bedroom. A roof only five years old, he says under his breath.

His hands were shaking so much he couldn't get the door unlocked.

Let me do it, I said. What if someone comes?

No one will come. The house isn't listed yet. It belongs to a woman who's gone to Singapore. She's a banker.

We went upstairs and pulled the covers off a bed. I let him do what he wanted. I won't even tell you. I turned my head so I wouldn't have to watch. When he went inside me I didn't like it. I hit him. I said hurry up. You don't even know what you're doing.

When he was finished he went outside to have a cigarette. You can't smoke in a house you want to sell. The smell lingers. For some people that alone is enough to kill a sale.

I went in the bathroom and tried to clean up. I could see him from the window, poking a little lily pond with a stick.

On the way home we stopped at a drugstore. He bought some chewable aspirin and a Coke for me and some breathmints for himself.

Mrs Green thinks I've quit smoking, he says. I'd appreciate it if you didn't mention that I have a cigarette every now and then. There's no point in getting her upset.

No, I said. I won't say anything.

He drove me back to Frank's. Mom came out on the steps to meet us. I was afraid she'd be able to tell what

I had done. I thought I'd have some look or smell and then she'd know, but she acted perfectly ordinary. She asked me if I'd had a nice time with Elizabeth, and then she invited Jack in for a drink.

I went upstairs and got in the tub. I could hear them talking in the kitchen. Every now and then somebody would laugh.

When I was clean I splashed Frank's cologne all over. That was a dumb thing to do. When Mom came upstairs she stuck her head in my room and took a sniff.

What is that stink? she says.

Chaps.

What happened? Did you spill it? Open the window. I can't even breathe in here.

She squints at me. Have you been smoking dope or something?

I have to laugh now.

Miss Paschonelle says I was raped.

I didn't want to hear that.

NO! I say.

Did you want him to have sex with you? Were you willing?

I must have been.

No, I don't think so. Did you enjoy it? Is that really what you wanted?

No.

Then it was rape.

I felt sick at my stomach. As if I was going to throw up.

I said you are not helping me feel any better.

She said I'm not supposed to make you feel better. I'm supposed to help you confront what happened. You were raped. Now you know it. That's why you feel so bad, Linda.

We left it at that. I never win any arguments with Miss Paschonelle.

Still I'm not sure we have got to the bottom of it all. Sometimes I think I know more about sex than she does. She was married only those two months, remember. We don't know what happened then.

I tell her someday I'm going to write a preliminary report about you.

11

Mom started work at Persic Realty the next week. She had to work in the office until she got her licence. She had her own desk in a cubby hole. She had me bring the boys down on a bus to see it. She wanted those other women in the office to know that she was a family person. I brought some of Stoppard's artwork along and we pinned it up on the wall.

She had her own computer. She showed me how it worked. Say you want a house forty years old with a dish washer. It throws up a list of every house like that in a given neighbourhood.

A house is the single largest purchase that most families will ever make, she says. We're here to help them make the right choice.

She showed us the xerox room and the place where they make coffee.

Look, she says. I've got my own cup.

She was so happy she almost dropped it.

We saw Jack at the office. He acted as if nothing had happened.

Hello, Mr Green, I say.

Hello, Linda. Hello, Stoppard. Come to see where your mother's going to work?

When we left he gave Stoppard a dollar so he could get a cone.

Thanks, Mr Green, we say. Have a nice day, Mr Green.

I thought that was that, but when I got home the phone was ringing.

When can I see you? he says.

My heart went right through the floor. Where are you? I said.

In my car. Up at the Mobil station. I followed you. I saw you and the boys getting off the bus. Can you get away?

No! I said. What are you talking about?

I have to see you, Linda, he says. I have to.

I took the boys over to the Seymours' next door. They are a retired couple and would help out in a pinch.

Oh, Mrs Seymour, I say. Can I leave the boys with you for a second? I have to run over to the Krogers.

Want me to drive you? Mr Seymour says. He was bored with his retirement and always looking for something to do.

No, no, no, I say and run out the door and up the street toward the Mobil. I could feel my face turning bright red. I was sure they knew exactly what I was doing.

Jack was waiting in his car. We went someplace. I don't even remember where. We parked by the river, I think. I was gone about thirty minutes. When I got back to the Seymours' I was still sweating. I felt like I hadn't breathed right since the phone call.

What did you want at the Krogers? Mrs Seymour says.

I don't remember. Baking powder.

Well, I've got that right here, Linda. You should have asked me.

They are nice people. Mrs Seymour is into coupons and keeps them in a special box on the kitchen counter. They are arranged according to expiration date, and she grabs a handful when she goes to the store.

Mr Seymour thinks she buys things they don't need. For example, a twenty-five-pound bag of dog chow.

We don't even have a dog, he says.

It's a gift, Arnold, she says.

Who for?

I don't know yet.

He had to take a walk around the block and cool off. Mrs Seymour closes up her coupon box and puts her hand over her eyes.

When I think of the sacrifices I've made, she says.

Miss Paschonelle wants to know how often I saw Jack. She has her pencil ready. She wants to write down a number.

I don't know. I didn't keep count. It wasn't that many times, really. It was hard for me to get away. We'd make arrangements, and then Mom would have to go out at night with a client or Frank wouldn't show up when he was supposed to and I'd have to stay home. I was afraid Jack would start to hate me, but he never did.

It was hard to find a place to go. The best places were the houses that he had for sale or rent. The ones that still had furniture. He wanted clean sheets and towels. They had to be exclusive listings so no one else would show up. Some were really nice. After he was finished, I liked to prowl around and look in all the drawers or work the kitchen appliances. Some people had incredible junk.

One house had a lap pool. You threw a switch and the water started to flow. I swam in there until I nearly drowned. Jack had to practically drag me out. That was my favourite house. I really wanted to go back there again, but he sold it to a couple who designed the software for the evening weather show.

Another house belonged to an old lady who died of old age in Arizona. Her drawers were filled with old dresses. I used to put them on and dance around. They were too big and the tops hung down. Jack didn't like that.

Stop it, Linda, he says. Put those dresses back where you found them. They're not yours.

What he was really worried about is that I would leave a trace. Before we left he would pull the sheets off the bed and gather up the towels so they could be washed at the laundromat and people wouldn't know what had happened in their house. He was so neat and tidy. Hiding everything away. I started to hate him a little for that. I wanted to leave clues. I wanted people to know about us.

I sat in a chair and watched him clean. The chair was upholstered and he got a towel to put underneath. He was afraid I would leak.

No! I said.

Don't be difficult, Linda.

Why did you sell that house with the lap pool?

I had to, Linda. It wasn't my house. You know that.

I thought you loved me.

I do, he says. I do love you.

If you really loved me you wouldn't have sold that house with the lap pool.

Please, Linda, he says. Please. He had to calm me down then. Sometimes it would take hours. I was pretty immature. He had to put up with a lot. Almost anything could set me off.

His mobile phone would beep every ten minutes. He had to answer it. It would be suspicious if he didn't. Once it was his wife. Elizabeth wanted to go to a movie that didn't get out until ten-thirty.

Jack said no. It's a school night. She has to be in by nine-thirty. She knows that.

Mrs Green must have given the phone to Elizabeth because I could hear her begging at the other end.

Jack wouldn't budge. He says you know the rules, Elizabeth.

When he hangs up he looks at me.

Sorry, Linda, he says.

Get away! I yell. I wouldn't let him touch me for weeks. We'd go sit somewhere in the car. We'd watch football practice at a high school in the suburbs. Nobody noticed us. We behaved. He'd try to hold my hand. Keep away from me! I'd say.

Eventually he found an apartment on Bryant Street we could use, and that's where we would go. It belonged to the company. Some college students had trashed it and it couldn't be rented until it was fixed up again. Jack pulled the work order so nobody knew about it anymore.

In effect, he says, this apartment no longer exists. We can stay here as long as we like.

He bought a microwave and a TV. We'd eat burritos and watch old movies. It was nice, but I wasn't sure I wanted our own place, even if it didn't exist. I missed going to other people's houses. I missed the old dresses and the indoor barbecues and the lap pool.

It's so boring here, I said.

*

Mom got her realtor's licence in August. She sold two houses the first month. She showed me the cheques. Her commissions. They were for thousands. She leased a car and bought new clothes.

I said you want me to look after that money? I could invest it for you.

She just laughed. She said I think I can manage it myself.

I thought we were going to get rich on real estate.

She had friends we didn't meet. She said she was embarrassed to bring them to the house. When she came home she smelled like Mexican food. Like cigars. I dumped Tyler in her lap and Stoppard crowded up close. She pushed him away.

Linda! she says. Do something with these kids! They're all over me.

Frank told her she shouldn't ask me to do so much child care.

She hated that.

What do you know? What do you know about it? Someone has to make a living around here.

She would leave then and not come back for hours. We didn't know where she was. I didn't care. It was calmer when she wasn't around.

The weather stayed warm right into the fall. I sat out on the lawn with Tyler and Stoppard and ate apples. We watched Frank rake the leaves around the cut-out cows. No one was buying any, and the paint was starting to come off. The wedding date came and went, and nobody said a word.

*

Frank started coming into my room at night. He'd sit on the edge of the bed and talk.

Did you see those Knicks? he says. They were down eighteen points and still won.

He squeezes my knee through the covers.

Yeah. That's great, Frank.

He shakes his head. No it isn't. I had twenty bucks on Chicago.

He wanted to know if I thought Mom was sleeping with Jack.

No, I don't think so, Frank. He's not her type.

You have to wonder though. They spend a lot of time together. It's the nature of the business.

No, I don't think so.

Your mom could have had any man she wanted. Any man at all. That's the problem. And she chose me. You have to expect a little friction.

I said things will be OK, Frank.

Yeah. After we get married, things will settle down.

He lets go of my knee and looks at his hands. I almost sold a cow today, he says.

I tried to talk to Jack about him. I said can't you give him a job, too?

I don't know, Linda. What's he going to do?

We were in our little apartment on Bryant Street. I said why don't you let him fix this place up and pay him a lot of money?

Oh, Linda, he says. Bag of bones. Will you stop trying to be nice to everybody?

He wraps me up in his arms.

This is our special place. Where could we go if Frank was hanging around?

Mom met a married couple at a real estate seminar on marketing for the retirement years. Their names were Timmy and Micky. They had the same colour red hair and looked like twins. They spread out their papers on the kitchen table and talked about an infomercial they were putting together. I think they were real crooks. They wanted to gyp old people. They had some flashy pictures they were handing around.

Frank didn't want Mom to get involved. He was hostile to the idea. He said those look like fake pictures to me.

Micky says they're not fake, Frank. They're computer generated. To show investors what the concept looks like.

You mean they are fake, then.

It's virtual reality, Frank.

Timmy says what do you do, Frank?

I have my own business. Lawn ornaments.

Lawn ornaments? Is that those animals in the front? You make them yourself?

Yes.

You hear that, Micky? Frank's in lawn ornaments. Maybe we could tie it in somehow.

Micky looks at Frank. I don't think so, she says.

Frank says why do you guys dye your hair the same colour? Is that virtual reality?

When they left, there was a silence.

Mom tried to pick up the folders that Micky and Timmy had left, and they fell on the floor.

She said I'm not going to forgive you for this, Frank.

I'm not going to forgive you. She turned around and walked out the door.

That night when Frank came up to my room he was drunk. He had that magazine where he first learned about the cut-out cows. It was all tattered and falling to pieces.

Look at this, he says.

I already saw that. You showed me.

But read it again. The highlighted part.

J. P. Dimwiddy of Carlyle, Pennsylvania grossed four thousand three hundred dollars in his first month using the PressEase patterns for creating adorable livestock . . .

He pushes the magazine down in my lap. Do you know how many I've sold? he says. Four. And two of those to Jack Green.

But that's over six hundred dollars. That's good.

Yes, he says. That's all right. It's a beginning.

Yes. It's a beginning.

He stares at the pictures in the magazine and sways back and forth. Your mom isn't going to come back, he says.

What are you talking about, Frank? She was going to Detroit for a meeting. That's all. You knew that.

He shakes his head. This time I didn't feel a thing when she left, he says. Not a thing. I don't even want her to come back. We're fine without her. Just you and me and the boys.

He took the magazine and smoothed it out on my knees.

No one's buying any of the cows. They'll buy chickens, but I can't make any money off of chickens. I can't charge as much. They're harder to make, but they're little. It's the cows where the money is. I'm not selling any cows.

It'll be OK, Frank.

No, I don't think so. I'm going under, Linda. Right before your very eyes.

He grabs my hand and squeezes until I thought the bones would break. It was a real relief when he went away.

I heard the band saw out in the garage start up. I thought he must be making more cows, but he wasn't. He was cutting up all the livestock into little puzzle pieces. When he was finished, he dragged them into the house and tried to burn them in the woodstove down-stairs. It was a little cast-iron thing that he'd stuck in the fireplace. It was too small for what he was trying to do. Soon the house was full of smoke. It smelled like burnt paint. I got dressed and then I got the boys out of bed. We went out and sat on the steps. I was afraid Frank was going to set the whole place on fire.

Mr Seymour came over in his bathrobe and said he was concerned.

There's smoke coming out the window, Linda, he says.

It's OK, Mr Seymour. The stove pipe got a leak. Frank's going to fix it.

He just shook his head and went back into his house. I could see the light in his kitchen come on and he's shaking his head at Mrs Seymour.

I left the baby with Stoppard and went in and told Frank. I said come on, Frank. Don't do that. Mr Seymour's going to call the police if you don't stop.

I tried to shut down the damper on the stove, but he pulled me away. We sat down hard on the floor. He wrapped his arms around me and started to squeeze.

132

Oh god, Linda, he said. Oh god.

I could hardly breathe. I said don't, Frank. Don't do that. You can burn up the stuff. I won't stop you.

We rolled over on the floor and I tried to get away, but he wouldn't let me. He pulled up my shirt and started wiping his face on my stomach. I could feel the slobber on my bare skin.

I banged him on the ear and he let go. I got as far as the door and then he came after me again and got me down again in the front yard.

I said let me go, Frank. I won't tell anybody.

I was really scared.

He says no, that's all right. Everything's all right now.

He pulls me up on my knees and tries to brush off the dirt and leaves.

He said do you know any prayers?

The our father one.

Say it.

Our father who is in heaven . . .

I could see Mr and Mrs Seymour watching us out their kitchen window, and Stoppard came down the steps with Tyler in his arms.

It's OK Stoppard, I said. Take Tyler and go over and see Mrs Seymour.

When I got Frank calmed down a little, we went in the house and shut down the dampers on the stove and opened the windows.

I said I'm going next door with the boys, OK?

He shakes his head.

That son of a bitch gets everything he wants.

Who, Frank? Mr Seymour? He doesn't have anything.

No, he says. Not him. He gives me a hug. That's all right. Go to bed, Linda. Go over to the Seymours'.

The boys and I spent the rest of the night next door. We slept in the guest room. A king-sized bed. It was too big. You couldn't find the edge. I felt lost.

12

Mom came back from Detroit the next day.

I think I've lost all my money, she said. Or most of it. Those bastards.

She meant Micky and Timmy. I never found out what happened. It was the infomercial, I think. She invested in that. I don't know if she was robbed or what. Maybe she is still waiting for a return. That would be reasonable, but she might not know it.

She picked us up at the Seymours' and drove us to the place where we live now.

We're going to live here for the time being, she said. Just until we can afford something better.

Stoppard and I walked around the rooms. They looked good empty. The sun was shining. The floors were dusty but otherwise clean. I put Tyler down on my jacket, and he sucked his toes.

How did you find out about this place? I said.

From Jack. It's a rental unit. It belongs to Persic Realty. I got the key at the office.

Why didn't we move here before? I said.

Listen, Linda. We're here, aren't we? I'm doing my best.

She went over to Frank's in the afternoon and got our stuff. I don't know if she told Frank she was coming or even if he was there. Maybe she didn't say anything at all but just went around his house grabbing up T-shirts and socks and jamming them into plastic bags. That's how they arrived. All mixed up. Even some wet clothes from the washing machine stuffed in with some dirty sheets. Everything stank of mildew and smoke.

I said why didn't you put the wet stuff in the dryer first?

I didn't want to negotiate, she said. You can wash it again.

She went out and bought Mexican take-out for supper. We used the radiator that ran under a window for a table. We could stand there and look out at the people in the street while we ate.

This place isn't so bad, she says. We could be quite comfortable here.

After supper we went out and bought some furniture. The fold-out couch and a couple of mattresses. Also the TV. She wouldn't pay unless they promised to deliver that night.

She put the whole bill on a company credit card. That scared me. When I got her alone I said what are you doing? You can't use that credit card.

She had some story. About how the furniture really belonged to Persic Realty and we would leave it in the apartment when we left.

I know what I'm doing, Linda, she says.

The next day we found a day care for Tyler two blocks away called Tiny Tots. Mrs Johnson runs that. I could pick him up there after school. Also Stoppard got home from school an hour before me, and she'd let him wait in her hall with a book until I came.

Sometimes if I was late she'd get irritable. It was because of the insurance. If he breaks a leg who's going to pay? she says. She'd make him sit inside with his jacket on and get all sweaty. Then when we went outside he'd catch cold. But ordinarily I was on time, so there was no conflict. It looked like we were going to have a good family arrangement after all.

Frank came over a few times. He said he had a right to see the baby since he was the father.

I didn't want to argue. I let him in. I sat on the couch with Tyler on my lap and made him wave his hands at Frank.

Say hello to Frank, I said.

Frank said he'd decided to go back to school. He was going to take a course in computer programming at the community college. That way he could upgrade his skills. He thought he'd be able to get a decent job and we could get this mess straightened out. He was going to get the repairs on the house finished. Everything was going to be great again.

I mean we belong together, don't we? he says.

I don't know. I don't think Mom thinks so, Frank.

But you do, don't you? We'll get her to come around. He smiles. Remember those potato chips you used to buy? The mesquite flavoured? Weren't those great?

You want to talk to Mom? I say. She'll be home in a little while.

No, not yet. When I talk to Sandra I want to be dealing from a position of strength. You know what I mean? But what do you think about the computer course? You think that's a good idea?

Yeah, that's great, Frank, I say.

He never did enroll. After a while he stopped coming over. I thought he was probably gone for good.

Jack was glad Frank was out of the picture. He thought he could come over any time he wanted.

No! I said. I don't want you here. Not with the boys around. It's sick if you come over here.

He couldn't understand that. He says will you please try to be reasonable?

No! I say. Do you want me at your house? What about Elizabeth?

He shut up then.

I fixed up the apartment on Bryant Street the way I liked it. I dragged an old desk over by the window. I kept my papers there. All the old quarterly reports on the Vanguard Morgan Growth Fund.

Jack said what do you want for your birthday and I said office supplies. He took me to Office Max and said I could fill a basket. Not a cart, but a basket.

I bought a desk set that came wrapped up together in one package. Pen and holder, ruler, letter opener, stapler, hole punch. Scotch tape dispenser. Everything you could want on a desk.

I bought a dictionary and a world atlas and set them up between two bricks on the window sill. They looked businesslike there. That was the effect I was aiming for. I had two jars I washed out and brought from home. One for pencils and a baby food jar for paperclips. I could sit there for hours. Sometimes I did homework, but other times I just sat with my hands folded and looked out the window.

I said to Jack you got anything you want stapled? He'd look around in his briefcase until he found some papers. I stapled them on every side.

You little idiot, he says. I was happy then.

Mrs Green was the one who found out. One night she came to our apartment and said Mom was going to have to find another realty company to work for.

There's no point in pretending you don't know what I'm talking about, she says. I've looked at the accounts. He's given you almost two thousand dollars.

I think you must have made some kind of mistake, Mom says. Those were advances. I'm going to pay those back.

Mrs Green shakes her head. I don't want to argue. I'm just explaining the situation. It's got to stop. If Linda sees Jack again, I'm going to call the police. I don't want to do that, but I will.

Linda? Mom says. What are you talking about?

I'll tell them everything. About Jack. About the money. Everything.

Get out, you stupid cow, Mom says. Get out right now.

Mrs Green stops at the door to put her gloves on. I don't blame you, Linda, she says. But it has to stop.

When she was gone, Mom stood there and shook.

It's OK, Mom, I said. I won't do it any more.

She came at me then, slapping and screaming. What is wrong with you? she says.

Stoppard comes out of the bathroom with the baby yelling stop, stop, but she pounds away until she is worn out. Then she ran to the closet and pulled down the suitcases from the shelf.

Pack up your clothes, she says.

OK, I tell her. If that's what you want. I thought she was throwing me out, so I cooperated without any argument. I went in my room and stuffed my clothes in a garbage bag. I already knew where I was going to go. The apartment on Bryant Street. My papers and financial stuff were already there, and I thought I would just move in and live there by myself. I could just picture it. Getting up alone every morning and picking out the clothes to wear that day and then listening to the radio while I ate breakfast. I'd stop at the store on the way home and buy enough for supper, and then I'd sit down at my table and do my homework whether I felt like it or not. And if Jack or Mom came knocking at the door, I wouldn't even answer.

That was such an exciting idea I had to sit down on the bed for a minute and just think about it.

I could hear Mom raging around the apartment and the baby and Stoppard crying, but I didn't even care.

I don't need you, I said. I don't need anybody at all.

I don't think she heard me because when I came out of my room she was gone. All of her clothes and the boys' things were piled in a big heap on the floor or stuffed in her suitcase, but she wasn't there. The door was wide open and Stoppard was sitting on the couch holding the baby so he couldn't get away.

Where's Mom? I said.

I don't know, he says. She left.

I sat down on the couch and waited to see if she had just stepped out for a minute and was going to come right back, but she didn't. After a while I gave up and put everybody's stuff back where it belonged in the drawers and boxes. There didn't seem to be anything else to do.

I was so disappointed. I won't kid you. I was really ready to go out on my own.

When Mom finally came home, it was late and she'd been drinking. It was the first time in a long time, so you know she was upset.

She had a man with her. He had a coat with a fur collar and a green hat with a feather in it.

This is Mr Singer, she says. Tell Linda what you do, Mr Singer.

I'm a glazier.

He fixes broken windows.

Yes, he says.

That's all he does. Summer winter spring and fall. Tell her what you put on your hands when they get chapped.

Bag balm, he says. It's for cows.

Bag balm! Mom thinks it's so funny she nearly chokes.

I said be quiet. You're going to wake up Stoppard.

Where's Stoppard? Is he all right? Mom says. I can't breathe. I think I will lie down.

I told the man he should go home now, and we went down the stairs to the door together.

Wait a minute, he says. She said I could stay here.

No, you can't, I said. Go home.

I'm too drunk to drive, he said, but I closed the door on him anyway.

When I got back upstairs Mom was waiting for me in the dark.

Is he gone? she says.

Yeah.

She starts to cry. I'm sorry, Linda, she says. I lost my keys. I didn't know how I was going to get home. He gave me a ride. That's all it was.

That's OK. Do you know where the car is?

Yes. Listen, Linda. I never meant to leave you in Florida, she says. I never meant to.

No. I know you didn't.

No, no. Listen. I meant to drive around the block and calm down. I meant to check into a motel and calm down and then I was going to come back and get you. I was never going to leave you with that crazy old man. But when I got in the car I couldn't stop driving. You understand? I couldn't stop. I drove all the way to Georgia and I ran out of gas. A policeman gave me enough to get me to the next service area. I just couldn't turn around. Not right there on the Interstate.

I know. It's OK.

You have to stop, Linda. It's not right for somebody your age.

I got her calmed down finally. She kicked off her shoes and lay down beside Stoppard and I covered her up, clothes and all.

It's OK, Mom, I said. I don't hate you. I won't do it any more.

She closed her eyes.

I ran into Frank tonight, she said. He cut off all his hair.

She opened her eyes wide.

He wanted to know how you are, she said.

What did you tell him?

I said everything is great. Just great.

Did you say anything about Jack?

She closed her eyes again. I don't remember. I don't think so. Maybe I should.

Don't even think about it, I tell her. That is not an option.

The next day happened the way I told the police. I got up late and was in a hurry to get Stoppard to his bus stop. I put the baby in with Mom and told her she'd have to take him to day care herself.

Do you understand me? I said.

That was the last time I saw her.

I went to school. Jack's car was parked out in front. I could see him watching me in his rearview mirror when I got off the bus. I put my head down and tried to walk right by, but he got out and blocked my way. He said we have to talk and I said no, I don't want to talk about anything.

I could see Mr Bonham was frowning at us from the steps. He is the assistant principal at Arthur Murray, and he's very strict.

I said to Jack you've got to get out of here right now, but he said no, he wouldn't leave without me. If he was going to get arrested, it might as well be here.

I got in the car and we drove away. I didn't feel that I had any choice.

We went to the parking ramp because it is a place where no one bothers you. There were only a few cars parked on the top level.

He said a bunch of things. He said he didn't know until the night before that Mrs Green had found out about us. He wouldn't have let her come over to our house and talk to Mom if he had known that was what she was going to do. He said he was sorry about that.

He wanted to know how much Mom knew and if she was going to go to the police.

I don't think so, I said. I'll just lie if she does.

No, you won't. They'll get it out of you. Tell them the truth. I don't care any more.

We got out of the car and looked out over the edge. The wind was blowing. It sucked my breath away.

I don't want Elizabeth to know. That's what I worry about. Why don't we just run away? he says.

Are you serious?

Why not? We'll just hop in the car and go.

I thought about it. I will admit that. I thought about Mom and Stoppard and Tyler. I thought about what it would be like.

I don't think so, I said. I just don't think so.

I changed the subject. I put my elbows on the cement and leaned out. You can see a long way from here, I said.

Yeah, he says. All the way to the edge of the world.

And that's what we were talking about when Frank came up and shot him. The edge of the world.

I don't have anything else to tell you. I'm really sorry, but I don't know what else to say.

Sister Mary Joseph will tell you that I am adjusting well here at the Centre. She says I have a strong sense of order. You can give that free rein in this place. In the morning I have my routine. I get up before the bell and use the lavatory when it's still private. Then I get dressed. I keep my underwear on the top shelf of my locker. Some of the girls jam theirs in any which way, but mine is all folded.

I put the clean on the bottom of the pile, and during the week it rises to the top. My outside clothes I decide on the night before, so there is no groaning and complaining on my side of the room about not knowing what to wear.

When I talk about complaining, that's Beverly Kopinski I'm thinking about. She's got the bed by the window.

She says oh Linda, can I borrow your cardigan?

Where's yours, I say.

I got mustard on it last night.

You should have washed it out, I tell her. It would be dry by now.

Beverly says oh great, Linda. Why can't I be perfect like you and think of everything?

You remember she is the one who wants a favour.

She asks Crystal then, and of course Crystal drops everything and finds something for her to wear. That is the way Crystal is, but I find it irritating sometimes. When I try to boss her on this point she won't listen.

It's all right, she says. I don't mind.

Beverly says mind your own business. You just want to hog Crystal all to yourself.

Looking out for somebody is not the same as hogging them. This is what I would like to explain to Beverly, but I don't have the time. It would take for ever.

I am doing well in my classroom work.

The Centre gives each girl a zipper tote to carry her supplies in. Some girls leave theirs all over the place. Not me. Sister Mary Joseph says I am the only girl she ever knew who actually uses a pencil up.

I do try. I pick out a 2.5 from the teacher's jar, and I hold on to it. I don't start a new one until it is ground down too small to hold.

Then I go up and get a fresh pencil. I don't even have to ask the teacher. She knows I use supplies responsibly. When she sees me coming, she smiles.

The pencil sharpener is by the door. It has a nice smell of cedar wood and lead. When it gets too full of shavings I'm the one who notices, nine times out of ten. I empty it out in the wastebasket and then I sharpen my new pencil. That is so pleasant it gives me the shudders.

I have lunch every day with Crystal and Beverly. Beverly can't make up her mind what to eat, but I have the same thing every day. Tuna fish on white and a bag of ripple potato chips. Beverly says she couldn't stand to eat the same thing every day, but I have logic on my side. I made that decision once about what to eat, and now I don't have to think about it any more. That is a great savings of time and worry. Already at homeroom I am looking forward to sitting down with my tuna sandwich.

The three of us have our own place by the pillar in the lunch room, but somebody has to get there first. You plop down in one chair and save the other two seats with a sweater or a book.

I make it my job to get those seats.

Sometimes somebody gives me an argument. They say you can't save seats for other people.

Oh yes I can, I tell them. Those are the rules. First come, first served.

I grab the other chairs with both hands and hold on. I would not let go even if somebody punched me in the stomach. They know it is not worth the fight.

Sister Mary Joseph backs me up. She says I am coming out of my shell, which is a good thing.

*

As I said before, I don't know what else to tell you. I want to go home. I understand very clearly that it was a mistake to get mixed up with Mr Green. I won't do anything like that again. I'm ready to work hard in school and I understand the dangers of unprotected sex. I will say no to drugs. If there is some other requirement, tell me what it is.

I know Miss Paschonelle wants me to have more therapy, and I'll cooperate, but I do want to say one thing. I don't really think there's any point in hashing over my relationship with Jack any more. Nothing we can say is going to change a thing. He's dead. I'm sorry, but that's that. I don't know what else there is to discuss. The more we talk, the less real he seems. Miss Paschonelle has a man in her head who isn't like him at all. Some mornings when I wake up I want to scream. I want to say: we were talking on the parking ramp. Frank came up and shot him. Then Frank went and shot himself. These are the facts.

What more is there to say?

Author's Note

I do not write for children. I simply write. I do not write for adults. I simply write. I want others to read and admire my work; I want others to think about the things I think about, and be concerned about the things that concern me. That is why I write, but I don't write for others.

That I am a children's book writer is an accident. I began as an illustrator at a time when there was little to illustrate but children's books, and the illustrations of children's books were what I admired most. When I began to write novels, I wrote about young people, even if I didn't write for them. The style that comes naturally to me is rather straightforward and uncomplicated, and my work is easily accessible even to people who haven't read much, so perhaps it was natural that I should be thought of as a writer of children's books. I think of myself that way.

But I still don't write for children.

There are those, I'm sure, who find such an attitude irresponsible. That what is appropriate for an adult audience need not be appropriate for a child, and that a writer of children's books needs to take this into account.

And how is this to be done?

Children plainly think that books are sometimes

inappropriate for them. They are bored by a book or find it too complicated to understand. Sometimes they are frightened or disturbed. Sometimes they think the book is all wrong, or talks about things they don't want to think about.

I trust such judgements. No child who feels that way about one of my books should feel he or she has to read it.

But what about those books that children do like and read avidly – and yet are bad for them? Books that are like candy. Or poison.

I do not think my books can be of the candy sort, sweet and bloating. So if they are inappropriate for children in this way, it must be because they are poison. They must put ideas in their heads, and make them think about bad things. Maybe even do bad things.

And yet if my books are of this sort, what a seductive poison they must be. I have never had a person come to me and say, 'It was your book that hurt me. I was a good person until I read it.'

But what about their parents? Their teachers? Their governors? Don't you care what they think?

I do. I care very much. But as I've said, I do not write for them.

If I wrote *The Facts Speak for Themselves* for anyone it was for a girl named Star. I never met her. I was on a school visit, and the librarian told me that there was someone who wanted to meet me, but she wasn't in school. She'd been suspended for three days.

'What for?' I asked.

'Waving her bra around the cafeteria,' said the librarian, and we both laughed.

I saw the librarian a few years later and asked what had happened to Star.

'She's all right, I think. Had some hard times. A couple of kids.'

I'm afraid that Star will never read or even hear of *The Facts Speak for Themselves*. It really isn't important. Linda's life isn't hers. But if the book is for anyone, it's for Star.

Julie Bertagna

Exodus

As the waters rise, the old world is lost. But a new world waits to be found . . .

Mara's island home is drowning, slowly but surely, beneath storm-tossed waves. As the mighty icecaps melt, the Earth is giving up its land to the ocean – and a community, a way of life, are going to die.

But Mara has seen something extraordinary. Far out among the dizzying electronic information stacks of the Weave, there are hints of a New World – of cities built out of the sea and reaching high into the sky. Cities where desperate refugees can surely find safety.

In a terrifying gamble for survival, Mara and the islanders of Wing take to their boats in the ultimate exodus. Somehow they must find a new home in a world they no longer understand – a world where anything and everything is possible.

But Mara's epic quest becomes something even greater. An extraordinary journey into humanity's capacity for good and evil. And a heart-wrenching story of love and loss – and the triumph of the will to survive.

Thrilling, inspiring and deeply challenging – Mara's unforgettable story will stay with you long after the final page.

Mirjam Pressler

Malka

POLAND, 1943

Malka's world is changing. Jews are no longer welcome in Lawoczne, the town that has always been her home. Taunted by the children who used to be her friends, and with her family threatened by Nazi round-ups, nothing is safe any more.

Now Malka's mother knows she has no choice – she must take her daughters across the mountains to safety in Hungary, a place where Jews can live in peace. But escape proves to be far harder than they could ever have imagined.

Separated from her mother, Malka finds herself alone in a terrifying new world – a world ruled by hatred, fear and constant danger. Hiding in alley-ways and cellars, she learns to conceal herself from a pitiless enemy.

As Malka struggles to survive starvation, desperate cold and brutality at the hands of the Nazis, she is unaware that, miles away, a broken-hearted mother is searching for her lost little girl . . .

The extraordinary, shocking story of child's fight to stay alive during one of the bleakest moments of human history.